PLAIN SAILING

PLAIN SAILING

by

DOUGLAS CLARK

LONDON
VICTOR GOLLANCZ LTD
1987

First published in Great Britain 1987
by Victor Gollancz Ltd,
14 Henrietta Street, London WC2E 8QJ

British Library Cataloguing in Publication Data
Clark, Douglas, *1919–*
   Plain sailing.
   I. Title
   823'.914[F]   PR6053.L294

   ISBN 0–575–04055–6

Photoset by CAS Typesetters, Southampton
and printed in Great Britain
by St Edmundsbury Press Ltd, Bury St Edmunds, Suffolk

For
Rebecca Eileen

Chapter 1

DETECTIVE CHIEF SUPERINTENDENT George Masters and his close colleague of many years, DCI Bill Green, were walking along Oxford Street, passing Selfridges and heading towards the Circus. The pavements were well populated, the tourists of late May thickening up the home crowds, while the good weather seemed to have put a ban on hurrying. Progress was not rapid among the dawdling thousands, and the two detectives were obliged to jink, separate and then come together again, as they tried almost to bulldoze a way for themselves. They were, however, shoulder to shoulder in a few yards of clear space when a man's voice behind them said quite audibly, in tones with a strong trace of a northern accent, "It's not safe for cops to go out singly down here, love. They have to send them out in pairs."

Masters and Green exchanged sideways glances as a woman's voice replied, "I know, dear. It really is awful in London these days. Nobody's safe to put a foot over their own doorstep now."

At this, as if by pre-arrangement, both Masters and Green stopped and turned. A burst of laughter greeted the movements before Masters could say, "I thought I recognized the dulcet tones, despite your efforts to disguise them. How are you, Matthew? And you, Philippa? And, more to the point, what are you doing down here?"

Green was shaking hands with the couple, DCS and Mrs Cleveland, of the North Eastern Counties Force. The three men had worked together on a case in Nortown the previous December, and Philippa Cleveland had entertained the London men with unmatched northern generosity during their stay on her husband's patch.

1

"We are down visiting our son."

"Didn't know you had a boy," said Green. "I don't think you got round to mentioning him when we were up your way last year."

"We were too busy then," reminded Cleveland. "A little matter of a dozen murders to be solved doesn't leave much time for family histories."

"Is your son down here in London?" asked Masters.

Philippa answered, with no effort to disguise the pride in her voice: "He's an accountant now. He works in New Malden. Do you know where that is?"

Masters nodded. "Kingston way. But I'd never have believed you old enough to have a son mature enough to be a qualified professional man."

She laughed with pleasure. "Flatterer . . ."

"Talking of flattery," interposed Matt, "Jimmy has just bought one."

"One what? A flat?"

"And acquired a steady girlfriend," went on Cleveland. "Philippa thought the juxtaposition or coincidence of the two events could be sinister."

"Women have dirty minds," grinned Green.

"That's what I told her, but nothing would do but we had to come down here for ourselves to see how the land lies."

"He met her sailing," explained Philippa. "At the club. Jimmy always has been keen on sailing."

"He's good at it," explained Cleveland. "Started early, up our way, and joined in down here several years ago. They do a lot on the river and those reservoirs over near the airport, but he goes down Chichester Harbour way mostly, to get out on to the open sea, which is what he was used to up north."

"Sounds like a good, clean, healthy occupation to me," said Masters.

"And how have you found the situation concerning the girlfriend?" asked Green. "Everything all right?"

"Of course it is," retorted Cleveland. "As I said to Philippa, he's more interest in that Supranational of his than . . ."

2

"That's his boat," interjected Philippa. "Not a new one, of course. They cost thousands. But he's done it up beautifully. We've seen it."

"What I was going to say," said Cleveland tolerantly, "was that his big love affair at the moment is with his boat. I don't say the girlie comes a bad second, but she seems to understand his priorities and finds it perfectly natural that he's more interested in the cut of its jib than in the cut of hers, if you get me."

Masters grinned. "Priorities right and interests distinctly healthy."

"That's right. To put it bluntly, they're not living together and we've met her parents. They're the sort who keep a pretty watchful eye on her."

"Good."

"She's very nice," said Philippa. "And pretty."

"So now we can go home satisfied," said Cleveland with a grin.

"When do you go?" asked Masters. "Is there a chance of you both coming to have supper with Wanda and me? Bill and Doris would join us."

Cleveland shook his head. "We're catching the early morning train tomorrow and tonight we're taking the kids—Jimmy and Janet . . ."

"That's the name of the girlfriend?"

"Yes. We're taking them out to some Italian restaurant in Richmond they seem to be keen on. We're staying in Jimmy's flat, you see, and this is to be a sort of farewell party."

"Pity," said Masters. "But it's been nice seeing you again, Philippa, and you, Matt. Bill and I must push on . . ."

"Sleuthing?" queried Matt.

"Something like that. But please, when you come down again to visit your son, remember to let me know. I feel sure we could arrange to meet for a meal and a chinwag."

"I'd like that," said Philippa.

"In that case," said Cleveland, "it's a promise. Most likely for sometime in the autumn."

*

3

Green and his wife, Doris, were very frequent visitors at Masters' little house behind Westminster Hospital. Ever since her marriage, Bill and Doris Green had appointed themselves honorary parents to Wanda Masters and, consequently, honorary grandparents to young Michael Masters, her toddler son, though Green was, in fact, his godfather. It was a very close relationship which the Greens, considerably the older couple, cherished, but one which, to their great credit, they never presumed on.

A couple of days after the meeting with Cleveland they were to have supper at Wanda's Palace, as Green called the Masters home. Masters' wife had shown she possessed the knack of being able to turn what was nothing more than a cottage into a little haven of simple luxury. She had set out to provide such a place for her husband and son and had succeeded to the point where all who visited them marvelled at the comfort and just-rightness of the tiny home. There was no fuss about tidyness or how one sat in a chair. Callers just enjoyed it, and the Masters enjoyed seeing their friends do just that.

The Greens arrived at seven.

"The first really nice ones off my climber," said Doris, handing Wanda a small bunch of pink roses. "Just enough for your dressing table."

"Lovely. Thank you. Come in properly, William." This form of invitation was sometimes necessary because the tiny hall would not accept more than two people at once and so a third, should there be one, was often left teetering on the doorstep.

"I will when there's room," grumbled Green. "Why women always have to block the gangway defeats me. I remember once . . ."

"Is Michael in bed?" asked Doris, determined to stop her husband's reminiscence.

"Of course he is by now," asserted Green as Doris and Wanda moved through towards the dining room beyond which was the built-on kitchen. He shut the door quietly behind him. "So don't go upstairs peeking for a look at him

4

and wake him up accidentally on purpose."

Doris had turned to reply when Masters said, from the sitting room doorway, "In here, Bill. There's plenty of bottled beer, but perhaps you'd prefer gin."

"Gin'll do," grunted Green, as though he might have preferred whisky had it been offered.

Masters looked at him interrogatively. "Something wrong, Bill?"

"Not wrong, exactly," said Green slowly, accepting the proffered drink and taking an immediate gulp. "It's just that Doris has got a bee in her bonnet."

"Is it something you would like to talk about?"

"She'll tell you herself. When we're having supper, I expect."

Masters sat down opposite his colleague. "I see. A surprise in store."

Green merely grunted by way of reply, and the conversation drifted on to another matter about which Masters had wanted to consult Green. So it was, as her husband had foreseen, that when they were all sitting at table the bee was allowed to escape from Doris's bonnet. Masters started to entice it out as he handed her a plate of cold sliced chicken and ham. "Help yourself to salad," he suggested, "and then perhaps you might like to tell us whatever it is that Bill says you want to talk about."

"He hasn't told you?"

"No. Just that you have something to say, so I was clearing a space centre-stage for you."

Wanda was passing the salad dressing. "Is it something exciting? Oh, and would you like some of these curried potatoes? I can't say I've ever made them before, but I went to a buffet supper a few weeks ago and had them there. I enjoyed them, and I was told that they used to be widely used in naval wardrooms abroad at Sunday night parties."

Doris accepted the dish, and as she spooned some of the brown-powdered dice on to her plate, she said: "I've hired a cottage for a holiday, that's all."

"Hired?"

5

"Yes, I wrote away for one of those catalogues and chose a cottage I thought I would like out of it. I didn't get my first choice. That had already gone, but the one I have got is in a village called Stanhope. It's pretty, it's reasonably cheap and the village has a frequent bus service which I thought was necessary for Bill and me."

"Quite right," said Wanda. "Has it got all mod cons?"

"Apparently. It's built of stone and has been converted. It has a new bathroom and loo, an electric cooker, refrigerator, immersion heater, electric fires and open fires. The electricity is included in the price."

"It sounds ideal."

"Stanhope? That's north country, isn't it?" asked Masters.

"About twenty miles west of Durham, I think. I know the bus service goes to Crook and then on to Durham, and it's about an hour's ride."

Wanda asked: "Why there, Doris?"

"Because I've never been up in that part of the country," said Doris simply, "and I thought I'd like to go."

"What better reason could there be?" asked Masters. "Good for you, I say, Doris. You took the bull by the horns and booked the cotage. So what's the trouble? Is Bill proving difficult?"

Doris blushed. "He didn't know anything about it until I'd got it all arranged. Then I had to tell him because I wanted a cheque from him."

Masters grinned. "Is he feeling a bit umpty because he wasn't consulted, or because he had to fork out the deposit?"

"No . . . it's neither, exactly."

"What is it then?" asked Wanda. "Is there some other problem?"

Doris looked guilty. "Well . . . you see . . . well, I didn't book it just for Bill and me. I booked it for all of us."

"All of us? You mean George and Michael and me as well?"

"It's got the space," gabbled Doris. "I made sure of that. Beds for four people and a cot. A double room, a twin room and a little room for a child."

"But, my dear . . ."

6

"You're not angry, are you, Wanda? But you and George have entertained Bill and me ever so many times and I thought we'd like to do something in return."

"Of course I'm not angry, Doris. I'm absolutely thrilled and grateful, but . . ."

"But you don't want to come?"

"Of course I want to come. I shall come and bring Michael, but what I was going to say was that I can't answer for George. It will all depend on when you've booked it for."

"The wrong date is the only possible reason why I would not join you," said Masters. "I don't have to tell you, do I Doris, that I'm delighted at the prospect and by your thoughtfulness in thinking of us. There are mountains up there and Hadrian's Wall nearby and, as Bill will tell you, some jolly good pubs for eating in, and one of the things I've always wanted to do is to pay a visit to Durham Cathedral. It's supposed to be the most perfect building in the world. And that's not simply an English belief. A year or two ago an international jury of architectural buffs and archaeologists came to that conclusion, and . . ."

"Steady on, steady on," growled Green. "It's a holiday we are proposing, not a course of postgraduate lectures on St Columba or whoever it was who waved the big stick up there in the old days. Picnics, day trips and a breath of fresh air in the nearest Jordie chippy . . ."

"Just listen to that," said Doris. "And before we came here tonight he as good as told me I would be making a fool of myself by asking you to join us."

"Oh, my dear," said Wanda. "William didn't think we *wouldn't* want to come with you, did he?"

"Oh, no, no. Not that you wouldn't want to come with us. Just that you wouldn't want to go to a cottage when you usually go to a hotel."

"Those days are nearly over," said Masters. "Now that Michael is getting to the stage when he wants to run about and play with beach balls and be generally boisterous, it will have to be holiday cottages for us."

"That's right," agreed Green. "You can't take a handful

like young Nibbo into a hotel dining room. He'd have the Mississippi mud-pie down some memsahib's corsage before you could say Jack the Ripper."

"Mississippi mud-pie?" queried Wanda.

"We were in a hotel once," replied her husband, "where our waitress took great delight each evening, when telling over the contents of the sweet trolley, in calling the chocolate mousse—which seemed to be an ever-present member of the team—Mississippi mud-pie."

"It was always the same one," said Green. "I recognized it every night. And no wonder. With a name as revolting as that, nobody ever chose to sample it, and so it languished on the lower shelf, untouched and gathering dust day by day."

"What was that bit about a corsage?" demanded Doris.

"Nothing really, love. It just seemed a likely spot for a spirited lad to file away a plateful of unappetizing dun-coloured ooze . . ."

"What-coloured?" demanded Doris, outraged.

"Dun," replied her husband. "Dee, yew, en. No gee, or even gee-gee, so there was no reference to fertilizer either implied or intended."

"Bill!"

Masters laughed. "I can foresee us having a lively time, conversationally, on this holiday."

"If it ever eventuates," grumbled Green. "Any more of that spicy spud, love?" he asked Wanda. "I like it. Reminds me of Shakespeare's sonnet."

"Now what?" demanded his wife.

"Spuds are usually white," replied Green enigmatically.

"What's that got to do with Shakespeare?"

"'If snow be white, why then her spuds are dun'."

Wanda almost collapsed with laughter. Green caught her eye and winked. "Best tell her later, love."

"Tell me what later?"

"That Shakespeare never mentioned spuds," spluttered Wanda. "He said breasts."

"Breasts?" asked Doris outraged.

"Corsage, love," said Green. "Dun-coloured. Like the

8

memsahib's after a generous application of Mississippi . . ."

"Bill!"

". . . mud-pie."

Wanda recovered sufficiently to pass Green the potato dish. Masters asked: "What did you mean, Bill? If it ever eventuates?"

"You said just now that your acceptance depends on the dates of the booking. My missus has only taken it for one week beginning on the Saturday young Reed gets married to Muriel Clegg, and we've all promised to be present at the ceremony. We're supposed to be taking that igloo over by four o'clock in the afternoon and at that time we shall still be hunting the bride or kissing the slipper or whatever it is one does at wedding receptions these days."

"Charging the glass," said Masters. "That's the best game of all on such occasions. Charge and recharge. Sounds like something out of the Light Brigade."

"That's what it is for most bridegrooms," grumbled Green. "Into the valley of . . ."

"Bill!"

"Yes, love?"

"Will you stop galumphing and listen."

"Me, love?"

"Yes, you. It hasn't yet penetrated your head that Muriel's parents live in Nottingham, so that's where the wedding is taking place. When we're there, we shall be half way to the cottage."

"Maybe, love, but have you thought about trying to get from Nottingham to Durham after four o'clock on a Saturday? To say nothing of a twenty mile bus drive on top of that before you can even collect the key? Then there'll be the little matter of settling in and wondering what we're going to do about rations for Sunday. That'll be about eleven o'clock at night, I reckon. Maybe this village . . . what's its name? Stanhope? . . . is the sort of place where the grocers stay open all night. Maybe. But, from your description of it, I doubt whether there's anything more than a travelling bread van that calls twice a week. If you happen to be at home when it calls, you eat that week, but all I'm saying is I can't promise to enjoy a holiday where I have to wait until Wednesday for breakfast."

Doris looked crestfallen and turned to Wanda. "It was the only week the cottage was free. June the twenty-fifth until . . ."

"The thirty-second," supplied her husband.

Wanda looked along the table towards Masters who immediately took the hint.

"Bill would have some right on his side, perhaps, if he and Doris were going up from Nottingham to Durham by train. But they're not, are they darling?"

"No," said Wanda. "I haven't got round to suggesting it yet, but George and I had already decided to ask you both to travel with us up to the wedding. We shall go in the car and there's plenty of room for four even though we have got Michael's seat strapped in." Before anybody could reply or comment, she went on: "The ceremony is at twelve o'clock, so I think we ought to be able to get away from the reception at three—at the latest—without appearing rude. How long will it take us to get to Durham, George?"

"Stanhope, you mean?"

"Yes."

"Three hours, perhaps three and a half, but I don't think so. It's motorway all the way until we turn off somewhere just south of Durham. We should be there no later than half-past-six."

"Thank you, darling. So there you are, Doris. Phone the woman or whoever it is you have to collect the key from and say we won't be there much before seven. If you explain we shall have been held up by a wedding there'll be no problem. All women will put themselves out over a wedding."

"And while you're at it," said Green, "ask if there's a fish an' chip shop in the village, because we won't be able to go out for dinner with young Nibbo in bed."

"Good idea," said Masters, "and if we take a small hamper of essential foods to tide us over . . ."

"Like a litre of gin," said Green.

"Quite right. Thirst things first. But over and above the absolute essentials there can be a few desirable items like cornflakes for Michael's breakfast and a loaf of bread . . ."

"Leave it to us," said Wanda. "Doris and I will decide on priorities and then provide."

"That's fixed then, is it?" asked her husband.

"All except your leave, George."

"How long to go? Four weeks, about? I think I ought to be able to swing it with that much notice. But whatever happens, it won't alter the arrangements for the Saturday. Wanda and I will come up to the cottage even if I have to leave again on Sunday or Monday. Wanda will keep the car with her. All she will have to do is drop me at Durham or Newcastle station and I can get a fast train down if needs be. Then I'll come up again later in the week to help drive back. How's that?"

"Just fine, darling."

"It sounds a lot of work for you, George," said Doris in a worried tone.

"Those are only contingency plans for if the worst happens. I confidently expect to be with you all for the full week."

Green turned to him. "Thanks, George. We didn't intend to scrounge a lift . . ."

"You? Thank me? Dammit, man, you and Doris are providing us with a week's holiday."

"That's right, chum. And I don't want any nonsense about offering to pay half the rent. It's our treat. You provide the car, but we provide the cottage."

"And half the petrol," said Doris decisively.

Masters smiled at her. "If it will make you happy, Doris, but really . . ."

"There and back will be six hundred miles, and in a car like your Jaguar that means a lot of petrol. So Bill and I will pay our share."

"Thank you. Now what? More meat, anybody?"

Things went more or less as Wanda had foreseen and, after the wedding ceremony, the four adults and Michael were away from Nottingham soon after three in the afternoon. Masters had driven from London that morning and as in addition—though he had drunk sparingly at the reception—he had had more to drink than his wife, Wanda drove the Jaguar towards the Doncaster by-pass and then north.

"Map-read for us, Bill, please," said Masters, handing Green the road atlas. Not that directions would be necessary until the time came to turn off the motorway, but maps held a fascination for the DCI, and having one to consult would help to take his mind off the morbid fear he had of travelling in fast motor cars.

Masters was right in his belief because, though Wanda, a very competent driver, rarely dropped below the permitted seventy, Green kept up an apparently unconcerned running commentary about the places they passed. Races at Wetherby and Thirsk, the army at Catterick, Scotch Corner's links with history, and the like until finally he leaned forward to say to Wanda. "We'll turn off left just ahead, love. Up the B6275. It'll be prettier than this and in any case it's the shortest route. Old Roman road, actually. Dere Street, it's called."

Wanda followed his instructions, skirting West Auckland, crossing the river at Witton le Wear before turning left on to the A689 to run through Wolsingham to Stanhope. On this last few miles of the journey the westering sun was a bit troublesome as the car headed straight towards it, and it was still shining brightly over the hills to the west as Wanda drew up outside the house where—according to very precise instructions—Doris was to collect the key of the cottage.

This house door opened on to the pavement. The pleasant woman who opened it and who, besides giving Doris the key, told her the way to the cottage, added that she had turned the immersion heater on earlier in the day so that there would be a tank of hot water for baths.

"Will there be any ice in the fridge for my drink?" asked Green across the width of the pavement.

"There, now, I forgot all about ice. Just wait a minute and

I'll bring you some of mine to last you until you can cool things down a bit."

A minute or two later she handed Green a large, wide, thermos jug. "Just leave it in the kitchen when you go," she said, referring to the jug.

"I shall make it my business to see you get it back tomorrow morning, love," promised Green. "What time do you go to church?"

The cottage was number five in a short row on a steep little road slanting down from the market place towards the river. Wanda, carrying Michael, went in first with Doris while the men started to unpack the car. Masters was standing on the narrow pavement surrounded by suitcases and holding an armful of macs when Wanda reappeared. "It's like pins in paper, darling. Everything's so clean and nice. The stairs are a bit steep, but the rooms are very big—at least compared with ours at home. Do come in and see."

Wanda had not exaggerated. The bed linen had been laundered and ironed by somebody who knew her business, and all the little things were there, including a cache of spare light bulbs and toilet rolls, with a stock of neatly folded tea-towels neighbouring the modern sink unit.

"Everything here," grunted Green after poking about for a minute or two. "Where's the box with the booze in it?"

Green busied himself with putting bottles of tonic and white wine into the fridge, filling the ice trays, selecting glasses from the cheap but cheerful collection provided and, finally, pouring drinks for everybody. By this time Michael had been changed into pyjamas and brought downstairs for a late but light supper which Doris had heated for him on the electric stove. They all gathered round the child while he ate at the table in the kitchen.

"That smells so good," said Green, "that I'm beginning to hope the choker can't eat it all, then I can finish it for him."

"Macaroni cheese," said Michael, looking up at Green. "And yoggit."

"Yoghurt, darling," corrected Wanda.

"Raspberry yoggit," said her son, and fell to clearing his

13

first dish in anticipation of the second.

Masters, who had wandered into the sitting room now came back and said: "Have a look at these, Bill. They may give you some ideas." He handed over to his colleague a sheaf of leaflets and brochures which he had found on a shelf in an alcove and had glanced at before passing them on.

Green took them and started to turn them over. "What are they, Bill?" asked his wife.

"Advertising gup and timetables and so on. Places to go and visit. Railway museum, stately homes, cathedrals . . . ah! now here's a little beauty. Places to eat. There's a pub at Fir Tree, that village we passed through before we turned left, another at . . . ah! We *have* got a chippy in the village. *And* it's Chinese. Who Flung Whatnot, specialist in fish and chips and English dishes. I wonder what your actual fish and chips are if they're not an English dish?"

"There's a visitors' comments book here," said Masters. "It gives the chippy a very good word. Somebody here has said that the takeaway steak and onions is very good and his wife liked the sausages." He looked up. "Does that sound as if it offers? At any rate for tonight?"

"It would save cooking," said Doris.

"I think so," agreed Wanda. "We've got quite a lot of tinned food and fresh tomatoes and eggs, but there's tomorrow night to think of and we may not be lucky enough to find a shop open on a Sunday."

"Say no more, love," said Green. "George and I will become a scavenging party while you girls put the nipper to bed and unpack your smalls."

"We'll leave it to you what you bring," said Doris, "but don't bring home a load of pickled eggs and gherkins and things like that."

"English dishes only?" asked her husband.

"Yes. Sensible things."

As the two men left the cottage, pulling the door shut behind them, a dog sitting on the opposite side of the narrow road got up and came towards them, tail wagging and tongue hanging out.

14

"Border collie," said Green. "Sheep dog." He stopped to pat the black and white animal. "Hello, mate. You're a nice, friendly sort of feller. What's your name?"

"'T ain't a him, it's a her," said a local man who suddenly appeared out of a passage gate close by. "Name's Nel."

"Is she yours?" asked Masters, fondling the animal's ears.

"Belongs to missus up top," replied the man. "She'll be out, I reckon. Nel allus comes down to welcome visitors to the cottages."

"Isn't that strange in a working dog like this? I thought sheepdogs were one-man animals and didn't really make good pets."

"Nel don't work. Leastways, not with sheep. Friendly old thing, she is. Sits about here for hours waiting for a word."

"Should she be out alone, not on a lead?"

"Her never goes out of the street, do you, Nel? Her'll be here when you get back."

"Talking of getting back, chum," said Green, "could you tell us the way to the chip shop?"

"Up on to the main road at t'market and turn left. You'll see the sign a hundred yards along on a lamp post. It points to the chippy down a little side road opposite."

"Thanks."

As they went along, Green said: "They've got their priorities right here. Signposting the way to the local chip shop."

"You know," said Masters as they cut diagonally across the market square, "this isn't a village, it's a town. See here, bus stands and shelter, and I think we've got a castle or something like it behind that wall."

Green grunted. The steep climb had left him no breath for further comment.

"Newsagent and tobacconist here," said Masters. "Not far to come for the morning paper. Ah! And there's a grocer and a pretty good looking baker's shop. All nice and handy."

As they went along the main road the beat and sound of rock music became increasingly noticeable.

15

"Saturday night disco," grunted Green, who by now had recovered his breath.

Then they saw the sign. A simple white finger-board bearing the ill-painted legend FISH AND CHIPS. It pointed, as the man who had given them directions had said it would, across the road and up a narrow side street. But what caused the two Yard men to grimace and exchange glances was not the fact that the building on the left-hand corner of the little street was the police station—Edwardian red brick, blue lamp and all—so much as the fact that it was painfully obvious that the disco was being held on the upper floor of the station. Apart from the noise, flashing lights and gyrating figures could be seen through the upper windows.

"That's one way of keeping the local youth under—or should I say over—your eye," grunted Green. "But at a hell of a price for anybody on duty in there."

"Keeps 'em off the streets, I suppose," said Masters philosophically. "It must be a very big building for a station in so small a place."

"Probably HQ for a large surrounding rural area," said Green as they crossed the road. "I can see and smell the chippy. Quite inviting, too."

It was a busy shop, but well run. Customers gave their orders at the head of the counter and then took their seats, in order, on benches at the back of the shop to await their packages. Everything was handed over in small, white paper carrier bags. Armed with four of these, Masters and Green were on their way back to the cottage inside a quarter of an hour.

"The bloke who wrote in the book about the chippy being good was quite right," said Green as he wiped his mouth on a paper napkin. "I enjoyed that. Now what's on telly? Something with policemen in?"

"Washing up," retorted his wife. "After that's done you can have some coffee."

Green got up and turned towards the window. A moment later he turned back to face them. "Any scraps left?" he asked. "Meat scraps, I mean."

16

"You're not still hungry?" snorted his wife.

"No, but Nel's still out there, watching the front door."

"Nel?"

"Come and look at her."

Nel must have noticed them crowding in the window. She stood up and, tail wagging, slowly made her way across the little street, never taking her eyes off them.

"I've got a small tin of stewed steak," breathed Wanda. "I wonder if she would like that?"

"And I was stupid enough to ask for scraps," said Green.

Green was making coffee in the kitchen when Wanda came down next morning in her dressing gown, shepherding Michael.

"Good morning, poppet. 'Morning, young feller."

"Good morning, William. Michael would like some milk, but I'm a bit worried about how much we have left for breakfast."

"No sweat," said Green, making a cup of coffee for Wanda. "The milkman's been. I caught him in the road and got two pints. He's going to leave us two every morning, unless you leave a note asking for more. Delivery at half-past-six. Pay next Friday morning."

"That's marvellous. Thank you." She half filled a beaker for Michael.

"Would George like a cup? I'm taking one up for Doris."

"I'm sure he'd love one. Have you used the bathroom, William?"

"All done, love. Beard erased, ears pickled out, hair combed. Water's nice and hot."

"Good. So Michael and I can use it."

"All yours, love. Oh, and by the way, Nel's still there. I had a word with her when I went out for the milk."

"You mean she's been out there all night? Sleeping on the pavement?"

"It looked like it to me."

"But won't her owner be missing her?"

"Haven't a clue, love, but she seems to have adopted us."

"I think we shall have to find out where she lives and take her home."

"Leave it to me, sweetheart." He picked up two cups of coffee. "I'll now go and do my chambermaid bit. Pity the morning is so dull. I was quite looking forward to seeing the sun on the hills."

"No sun," said Michael. "He's having a holiday." And then he added, "Like us."

In contrast to Sunday, Monday dawned bright and warm. As a consequence, the five of them decided to go much further afield than on the previous day. They returned, hot and happy, a few minutes after six. Wanda had begun to fret slightly lest Michael's bath and bed times were again going to be later than usual. Doris was arguing amicably with her husband as to whether the gammon steaks they had bought for supper should be oven-cooked or grilled.

The gentle curve in the steep little hill meant that the front of the cottage could not be seen from more than twenty or thirty yards away. As Masters eased the car round the slight bend, he swore aloud.

"Darling?" asked Wanda, startled.

"No need to ask, love. Look in front," grunted Green. "That little beauty spells trouble or I'm a Dutchman."

"Oh, no!" gasped Wanda as her husband braked the Jaguar to a gentle stop behind the white, be-striped patrol car planted firmly outside their door.

Masters put out a hand to touch his wife tenderly on the shoulder. "Carry on normally," he said quietly. "I'll attend to this."

As Masters opened his door, a young, uniformed constable alighted from the police car. "Excuse me, sir, but are you DCS Masters?"

"I am. What can I do for you?"

"Sorry to trouble you, sir, but the sergeant sent me down to find you and say there's an important message for you at the station."

"Have you any idea what sort of a message?"

"No, sir. I think there was a phone call and I was told to come and find you."

"When was this?"

"I've been sitting here for an hour and a half, sir. I was told to wait until you got home and ask you to come to the station, you not having a phone in your cottage."

Green, having ushered the others indoors, now joined Masters. "What's up, George? Been parking on a double yellow traffic warden, or something?"

"There's been a call for me at the local nick."

"At the disco hall?"

"I suppose so."

"It's urgent, sir, I think," said the constable.

"I'll come straight away. We're right in thinking it's the station up on the main road, are we?"

"Yes, sir."

"We'll be able to pick up a bag of chips to tide us over," said Green.

"The inspector will be waiting for you, sir," said the constable anxiously.

"I'll follow you up immediately. You get off now. I shall need just a minute to explain things to my wife."

Masters and Green went through the open door into the cottage as the patrol car began to turn in the road. Nel sat and watched it go and then slowly wandered over in the hope of following the two men indoors.

"Not just now, lass," called Green as he closed the door. "I took you home yesterday, and you should have stayed there." Nel turned quietly and forlornly to wander back to her vantage point.

"Darling, what is it?" asked Wanda anxiously as she sat helping Michael with his supper.

"I've no idea, sweetheart," replied Masters as lightly as he could in an effort to dispel the air of dismay that had descended on the company at the prospect of the holiday being disrupted, if not cancelled outright. "But I'll tell you something, my sweet. I'm not going up to that police station until I've had a sluice and a long, cool drink." He turned to

Green. "Bill, if I go up for a quick dip, will you do the duty steward bit? I'll be down in five minutes flat."

"I'm way ahead of you," said Green. "The gin's already measured, the ice broken out of its tray. All that remains is the insertion of a slice of lemon and a tonic top-up. But I'm coming with you, because you can't blink the fact that if authority has been combing the countryside for you it must be important."

Masters nodded his agreement.

"After you with the bathroom," said Green.

"Liversidge, sir," the local inspector said, introducing himself. "Chief Constable Pedder rang up shortly after two this afternoon to tell me to get hold of you. He said he would wait in his office until he hears from you."

"In Nortown?"

"Yes, sir. And a Mr Anderson from Scotland Yard called a bit later. He wants you to ring him as well. At home if after six. I think he's the AC (Crime), sir."

"That's him, son," said Green.

"I'll ring Mr Anderson first," said Masters. "Can I use your phone?"

"Yes, sir. If you know the number, just ask for it. They'll get it for you at the desk."

"Thank you. Would you mind going through to make sure that the call will be private? I don't want some eager young constable listening in because he thinks a call to the Assistant Commissioner must be exciting."

"Right, sir, but my people don't. . ."

"They're human, son," said Green. "Even I'm going to try to listen in." He ushered Liversidge out of his own office.

The call was connected almost immediately.

"Masters here, sir. I was given a message asking me to ring you."

"Quite right, George. Blasted nuisance that cottage of yours not having a phone."

"You'd still not have been able to contact me, sir. We've been out and about all day."

20

"What? Oh, yes. See what you mean. The point is, George, I've had Pedder on to me . . . yes, the CC of NEC . . . asking for your help."

"Specifically me, sir? I am on holiday, you know."

"You and your team. And before you get too steamed up, you'd better know that the son of DCS Matt Cleveland has been murdered. . ."

"Jimmy Cleveland?"

"His name is James, certainly."

"Lives down in New Malden?"

"Haven't a clue where he lives, actually."

"In that case, sir, where is his body? If it's in New Malden, it's our own job anyway. CC Pedder wouldn't be involved, except as a friend of Matt and Philippa Cleveland."

"You won't have to come back down here, George. The lad was up there sailing in some big trophy week. In the NEC area. So it's Pedder's own bailiwick. He's asked for you by name and I had no option but to agree. He'll give you the details. When I told him where you were he said you might be able to operate from your cottage. Speak to him and arrange it, George. And, incidentally, I've sent DS Berger and WDS Tippen up to you in your team car. They left before half-past-two with all your gear, so they'll be with you pretty soon."

"Thank you, sir. Is that everything?"

"That's the lot, George. Try not to be too long about it. I don't want you up there for ever."

"Officially I'm on leave till next Monday."

"So you are. I was forgetting that. We'll try to make it up to you somehow, George. Love to Wanda."

Masters put the phone down and looked at Green who was standing close in an effort to overhear both sides of the conversation. "Did you get any of that, Bill?"

"Most of it," acknowledged Green. "Matt Cleveland's Jimmy! God knows what Philippa will be feeling like. Judging by that chat we had with them in Oxford Street, she worshipped the lad." He sucked his partial denture. "I don't like this at all, George. It's going to be an emotional one. Emotional on the Cleveland side and emotional at our end, too. And not only because we know the people involved. In our own families. Doris and Wanda will accept it, of course, but they're not going to like having their little holiday spoiled by this."

Masters grimaced. "I'll have to speak to Alf Pedder now. Meanwhile, as the two sergeants are on their way here, they'll have to be found somewhere to sleep."

"Liversidge can do that. Shall I get him in?"

"Please."

As soon as Liversidge had been given his instructions and had again left the office, Masters picked up the phone and asked to be put through to the Nortown HQ of the NEC Constabulary. The speed with which he got an answer from the Chief Constable suggested that Pedder had been sitting waiting for the call.

"George Masters, Mr Pedder. I have been instructed by Mr Anderson to . . ."

"Yes, yes, Judder." It was a habit of Pedder's to call all Georges "Judder", a habit picked up in childhood in his northern home. "I fixed it with your AC. Has he told you what has happened?"

"Nothing more than the fact that young Jimmy Cleveland has been murdered at a sailing meeting somewhere on the coast up here."

"That's right. Cyanide."

"Good heavens! That acts so quickly that . . ."

"Right. And he was out on the water at the time so there's a hell of a mystery about the whole thing. I reckoned it is just your scene. As a matter of fact I'd decided you were the bloke most likely to sort it for us, but I had to hold back in case Matt . . . but I don't have to tell you. Anyhow he himself asked me to get you, and before you ask, I didn't prompt him."

"I shall, of course, do what I can, but surely your own people have had it in hand since it happened."

"Not so's you'd notice," said Pedder quietly. "Oh, they're doing this and that, but after Matt demanded you should be called in I told them to back pedal."

"And you're absolutely sure Matt asked for me personally

to undertake the investigation? I'm asking because it could be that if his son was poisoned a mile or two out to sea in a small dinghy, it need not have been murder."

"You mean the lad could have committed suicide?"

"It's a possibility we shall have to bear in mind, and I wouldn't think Matt would want the Yard prying into . . ."

"He was murdered," said Pedder firmly. "The lad he was crewing for swears there was no sign of young Jimmy doing away with himself and that he was in fine fettle right up to the time . . . look, George, this job is, after all, Matt's own. He's the DCS up here, and he wanted to get stuck in personally, but I couldn't have that. Not him looking for his own lad's killer. He couldn't be objective enough, Judder. A bit of paternal rage might creep in, if you know what I mean. Besides, Philippa will need him with her for a few days. The loss of her lad has just about . . . well, you can imagine the state she's in."

"I understand perfectly," replied Masters. "I have Bill Green here with me and the rest of my team is on the way to join us. Now what I need is briefing."

"I'll give you the details."

"When?"

"Tonight. When can you get here? You're about thirty five miles away as the crow flies."

Masters looked at his watch. Nearly half-past-seven. "Ten o'clock," he said into the phone.

"Not before then?"

"I have to wait for my people to get here, and I want us all fed and watered before we start. Besides, I'm very doubtful whether there's much I can do tonight in the way of interviews or visiting the scene, wherever that may be."

There was a moment of silence, obviously to allow Pedder to think. Then: "You've all been to my house, Judder. Do you think you could find it again?"

Masters chuckled.

"Sorry," said Pedder. "Damn stupid question. I'll expect you at ten. I'll have the local District DI here as well. He'll side you in this business."

23

"Thank you. What area are we talking about?"

"Wearbay. On the coast east of where you are now, north of the river mouth. You'll be able to get to and fro easily enough from Stannup."

"Stannup? Is that how one should pronounce Stanhope?"

"I don't know about how one should, but that's how everybody does up here."

"Right, sir. Ten o'clock at your house."

"That's it. And, Judder . . ."

"Yes, Alf."

"Matt Cleveland asked for you. He's got a great deal of faith in you, like we all have. But he wants to know how and why, and he's counting on you to be able to tell him. So am I."

Another silence while Masters digested the implied responsibility. He felt slightly annoyed that Pedder should have thought it necessary to spell the matter out.

"We shall do our best," he replied eventually.

"I never doubted that, otherwise we shouldn't have asked for you. I just wanted you to realize fully that it's not only Matt and Philippa that's . . . what I mean is, it's not an impersonal case for *any* of us. It's literally here, in our own homes and you, well, I suppose you could say you're our sort of champion."

"I think we realize the implications, Alf."

"Right then. See you later."

Masters and Green drove back to the cottage in silence. Nel, still on guard, seemed to sense the sombre mood and waggled her way slowly across to them, nose and eyes downcast.

"It's all right for you, lass," said Green. "Nobody's mucking your holiday up. Though, come to think of it, you probably wouldn't mind a bit of excitement." Nel raised her head within his hand and licked the underside of his wrist to show her agreement.

"And I had hoped and planned for this holiday to be so nice," wailed Doris, almost in tears when she had heard what the two men had to say.

"Look on the bright side," said Wanda.

"How do you mean?"

"As I understand it, William and George can work from here. Admittedly they'll be away a lot of the time, but you and I and Michael will still have our car, so we can get out and about, too. Then we'll all be here in the evenings."

Doris tried to smile. Masters put an arm round her shoulders. "We'll work something out, never fear."

"Too true we will," said Green, "but just at this moment can we think about food? George and I will have to be going as soon as the sergeants arrive. Certainly by nine at the latest."

"It's all ready," said Wanda. "It's a good job we bought that gammon while we were out." As they sat down at the table she asked: "Incidentally, where are the sergeants going to stay?"

"Mrs Liversidge is giving Tip a bed. They've got a spare room she can have. Their daughter's, I think. She's away on holiday somewhere. Berger is going into a boarding house up on the main road, just two or three minutes away on foot."

"And don't forget, you lot," said Green, managing to say the words at the same time as he forked a slice of tomato into his mouth, "this place is called Stannup."

It was a minute or two before eight o'clock when the Yard Rover arrived at the cottage door. Hastily, Masters explained to Berger the arrangements made for him and WDS Tippen and then sent them off to the police station where they were to meet Liversidge who would see them into their respective quarters.

"I'd like you back here by nine at the latest. Earlier if possible."

"Right, Chief."

"Have you eaten?" asked Green.

"Not so's you'd notice," replied Tip.

"There'll be sandwiches here for you, lass. Both of you, get here as soon as possible so's you can eat them in something like peace before we set out."

"Where to?"

"Nortown, love. For a briefing."

*

25

It was still light as the Rover entered the outskirts of Nortown. Berger, who was driving, said: "I'll have to go to the city centre, Chief. I can find my way from there."

Green added: "I've only been to Alf Pedder's pad in the dark, so I'm not too sure myself, but I know we have to go straight on at the lights near the station and then go right, uphill, after about a mile."

"Quite right," said Masters. "And then . . ." He proceeded to detail the exact route to the Chief Constable's house where, a few minutes before ten, they drew up alongside the pavement. The short driveway was already occupied by three cars, leaving them no room inside the gates.

Pedder let them into the house. "By the Lord Harry," he said with relief in his voice, "if I'd been told a year ago that I'd be pleased to see four Jacks from Scotland Yard standing on my doorstep, I'd never have believed it. Come in, Judder, and you, Bill, and . . . what's this? A girlie?"

"In your vernacular I suppose you'd call her a Jill," replied Masters. "Actually she is WDS Tippen, known to all and sundry as Tip. DS Berger you already know."

"Of course. Glad to see you, son. Lost your mate have you? Reed, wasn't it?"

"He's been promoted, sir."

"I should think so, too. Now, all of you, in here."

He ushered them into the sitting room which the three men from the Yard remembered as the scene of the victory party after their success in the first enquiry they had been asked to undertake for Pedder. Two men were already there, their faces familiar, also remembered from the previous visit.

"You know Sandy Finch, one of Matt's DCIs and Ashley Head, the DDI of the patch with Cullermouth in it."

"Cullermouth?" enquired Masters. "I thought earlier you mentioned Wearbay?"

"It's the same place, almost," said Head, shaking hands. "Cullermouth is just the part where all the sailing's done and so forth. Wearbay is the big seaside resort just north of it, but it's all one. Conurbation you might say, I suppose."

26

Finch approached to shake hands. "Come to sort us out again, Mr Masters, have you?"

"To help, if possible," replied Masters, remembering how proud and intolerant of interference he had found these northern officers. He appreciated how much it cost them to ask for help from a Yard man, let alone work under his direction.

"We're glad to have you, sir."

"That's what I say, too." Head grinned at Green. "I was a mite suspicious of what I thought was your airy-fairy approach and fantouche theories at one time. But after you proved how right they were I changed my mind. And we're going to need some such ideas to work on now, because as far as I can tell, this job looks like being a fair bastard."

"Ladies present," murmured Finch in an aside to Head. Tip happened to overhear it. "Only policemen," she corrected.

"Sorry, all the same," said Head.

"Everybody sit down," ordered Pedder. "On the floor if there aren't enough seats."

"Got your shorthand pad?" Masters asked Tip quietly.

"In my shoulder bag, Chief."

"Contrary to my earlier reservations about note-taking, I'd like you to get this down. As much as you can of the relevant bits."

"Yes, Chief."

Pedder began. "I'll just fill in the background because I know you people from the Yard set great store by knowing the colour of the local bus-driver's socks before you set out on a job like this.

"Jimmy Cleveland was twenty-six and a bit. He was a clever lad at school and after he left he took up accountancy and did pretty well at it. He'd passed all his early exams and got enough qualifications to take on good jobs in the financial departments of big firms. All he lacked, as I understood it, was that bit of job experience that companies like their money men to have before they take on the really responsible

27

positions. He was, of course, still studying for even higher qualifications.

"He played a bit of rugger, too, but ever since he was about fourteen he had had a passion for sailing dinghies. He learned the rudiments of it in the Sea Scouts, I think, and then he sailed with a number of clubs round here that believe in encouraging junior and student members."

"Where?" demanded Green.

"Where?"

"Yes. Where did he sail as a choker, before he went south?"

Pedder looked at him hard. "Oh, I see," said the CC at last. "You've got it in mind somebody at one of those clubs could have had it in for him."

"You say he was murdered. Somebody must have had a pretty serious grudge against him. Presumably somebody who wasn't a stranger to the lad."

Pedder nodded his head. "If you think it's important to know where he sailed, then it probably is. Sandy will get you a detailed list, but I know he sailed with the local club on the river here and with another on the Derwent reservoir."

"That's somewhere just north of Stannup, isn't it?"

"That's right. Now, to push on. Young Jimmy sort of graduated through the classes of dinghy, from Cadets and Mirrors through National Twelves and the like till he got to what most of these sailing types consider the top. He joined the Supranational crowd. As I understand it, this is in every sense an international class. What happens is this. At every biggish club, like the one on St Mary's reservoir at Staines and the one at Itchenor on Chichester Harbour, there is a Supranational section. Six, eight, maybe a dozen dinghies. The people who sail them belong to the clubs where they are normally berthed, but over and above that they belong to the National Association of Supras, as they call them. They have a quarterly magazine of their own and every weekend one or other of the sections has some form of open meeting. So these Supra buffs travel the country, trailing their boats, a hell of a lot—Grafham Water near Bedford, Rutland Water, the east

28

coast near the Crouch, that new boating centre on the Trent at Nottingham and so forth."

"Every weekend?" asked Berger.

"Practically every weekend, son. Winter and summer alike. They even have daft races round Christmastime called the Icicle and the Frostbite and such like. One's called the Bloody Mary, according to Matt. Anyhow, the point is that we've established that every Supra sailor, that's helmsman or crew member, is known to every other one countrywide, so there's no pinning down any specific area or small group of people as likely to be of more interest to us than any other."

Pedder paused for breath before continuing.

"To get more specific about this meeting at Cullermouth. Every year the Supras have what they call the King's Cup Week. Way, way back in the year spit minus one, King George the Fifth presented a cup for dinghy racing. In those days there were hardly any classes at all. But the old boy was a sailor himself and he wanted to encourage the sport, so he gave half a hundredweight of silver to be competed for by any two-handed craft that could stagger round a course. Now the whole business is much more sophisticated and there are race meetings with trophies for scores of classes. But the old cup was handed on by whoever was the governing body of the sport at the time to the—well, I suppose you'd call it the senior class of dinghy. Consequently, the Supras have inherited the trophy and have raced for it for a good many years now. Each year they hold the race week at one of a number of suitable venues. Matt recalls Jimmy going to Torbay, Pevensey Bay, Sidmouth and one or two other places in the past. But up here, in Cullermouth, we have a very thriving sailing club with quite a large Supra section among its members. Cullermouth has never hosted King's Cup Week before because most of the other people were a bit wary of the weather up here. They didn't believe they could get a week of decent weather in the north-east without the wind whipping up the water so much as to make racing either impossible or dangerous.

"They were probably right about that, but there was

another thing. As you can imagine, to host a meeting like this calls for facilities that not everybody has. Clubhouse, hotel rooms nearby, car park at the beach, secure boat park, launching ramps, food, chandlery . . . you can guess the list is endless." He turned to look directly at Masters. "But a couple of years ago, the Wearbay Club built itself a new clubhouse at Cullermouth. I'll not describe it to you, because you'll see for yourself tomorrow, but it's good. And they made sure they had all the other facilities, too, together with a great raft of seaside hotels on the doorstep in Wearbay.

"So the lads up here were in a good position to demand that they should be included in the list of host clubs for the King's Cup. And this year—this week—is their first time of doing it."

"And now this tragedy."

"Right. You should know that boats come from all over the world to compete in the King's Cup. From Canada and the States, Australia, New Zealand, South Africa and anywhere else you can name except Switzerland and Outer Mongolia. That's one of the reasons why the meeting hasn't been cancelled. It's going on regardless, with everybody's blessing, including Matt's.

"I've mentioned these overseas competitors because it was a doctor from the States, who was helming his boat with his daughter as crew, who answered the call for help when Jimmy's helm started raising the alarm. And it was he who gave the first snap diagnosis of cyanide poisoning and who summoned the rescue launch to get Jimmy ashore smartish. Too late, of course. The lad was dead by the time they reached the beach. The doc did what he could, but he had no kit. He tried to force seawater into him as an emetic to empty his stomach. He splashed water over his face and gave him artificial respiration. The rescue launch had a cylinder of oxygen and they tried that, too, but it wasn't any good. Cyanide acts faster than greased lightning, as you know, so even on dry land there's not much hope, but when the victim is stranded two miles out at sea in a sailing dinghy, there's no chance at all."

There was a short pause before Masters asked, "Has the initial snap diagnosis been confirmed?"

"Yes," said Finch. "By both the pathologist and forensic. They knew what they were looking for, and it was easy. The stink of bitter almonds, and they said there was typical pink staining of the organs. Then the American doctor had given them his observations—the lad unconscious, respiration difficult characterized by. . ." Finch consulted his notebook, ". . . 'short inspiration and prolonged efforts at expiration'. Then there was froth on the lips, glassy eyes, dilated pupils and . . ." Again he consulted his notebook, ". . . 'and a cyanosed countenance'."

Masters nodded his thanks for this information. "Anything more, sir?"

"Nothing. I told my people not to start detailed interviews."

"Timings and names, perhaps?"

Ashley Head said, "The boats got on to the water at nine o'clock—between about a quarter-to and ten-past, actually, because they had to queue up to go down the ramps. The race wasn't due to start until ten, but there was very little wind this morning and they'd need the best part of an hour to get out to the start line which was about two and a half miles out. The race started on time, I understand, but by half-past-ten young Jimmy was unconscious. He reached the shore just after eleven. We knew about his death within ten minutes. We informed DCS Cleveland immediately. He wanted to know how it had happened. So I had to tell him it had been diagnosed as cyanide poisoning. He ordered me to make sure, so I asked the coroner to order an immediate post mortem, which he did. As Mr Pedder said, the pathologist and forensic confirmed cyanide poisoning almost before I could get a cup of coffee down me."

"This was before lunch?"

"Just before a quarter to one. I told Mr Pedder who told the DCS who, as I understand, asked if you could take the case. I think the Chief Constable spoke to the Yard right away, didn't you, sir?"

31

"Before two o'clock," said Pedder. "Anderson agreed and ordered your two sergeants to join you straight away."

"Thank you. And now, names."

"Jimmy's helm was a chap of about thirty-five called Harry Martin," said Finch. "He's a married man with two small children. His wife and family are up here with him."

"Are they staying in Wearbay?"

"That's right. Most of them have wives, families or girlfriends staying up here. There's a lot of socializing goes on in the evenings, apparently. Discos, barbecues, prize-giving dinner. That sort of thing."

"The doctor who treated him—American, I think you said?"

"Dr Jason Humpelby MD. General practitioner, with his daughter Ravina who crews for him. She's a medical student."

"If his daughter is that old, he must be a man of mature years."

"Forty-nine, actually."

"Old enough to know his stuff."

"He appeared to. By that I mean he told me that cyanide was one of a few poisons where a proper antidote . . ."

"Meaning a specific antidote?"

"Oh, yes. That's what he said. Without it, he reckoned all other treatment would be useless. And he said that you can't give artificial respiration by mouth, that's why he used the ordinary method and tried the oxygen."

"Thank you. Thank heaven he knew enough to diagnose the trouble and not to use the mouth-to-mouth method, otherwise we could have had a second corpse on our hands."

"Do you want any more names, Mr Masters?"

"Not at the moment. But I would like a list of everybody there, helms, crews, administrators, hangers-on, together with potted histories. Ages, jobs, homes, countries of origin. Complete profiles, in fact. And any dirt you can dig up."

"Dirt?"

"Gossip. There's got to be a motive for this killing. What is it? Competitiveness with the will to win overriding all else?

Marital or sexual entanglements? I don't know, but in a close-knit group this big there are bound to be the usual jealousies."

Finch nodded his head in understanding.

"Motive, means, method, opportunity," continued Masters. "We've got to get all four and then add a fifth. Mechanics. That'll partly be covered by method, but not entirely, I suspect."

"Meaning what, Judder?" growled Pedder.

"Meaning how do you feed a dose of cyanide to a man isolated in a small boat out at sea? The obvious answer is that the helm, Harry Martin, fed it to Jimmy. But judging from the fact that you're not holding Martin, I suspect you think that's a bit too obvious. And, frankly, so do I. The last place to choose to kill somebody is where you are the only possible suspect."

"That's exactly what we thought."

"Besides," went on Masters, "if you were to poison somebody crewing for you in a dinghy, the obvious answer, once your victim is unconscious, is to jibe or heel the boat in some way so that the body tumbles overboard—having first made sure the life jacket was unfastened, of course."

"Would it sink?" demanded Head.

"It would with a pig of lead attached to it," growled Green. "If you were planning the business that well you'd make sure you put to sea with a chunk of extra ballast in the bilges. Easy enough to do for a sailor who could knot a rope round a lump of iron and his victim's leg with one hand, while the other was on the tiller."

Pedder agreed. "A window-sash weight," he said. "Dirty great long lump of iron with a hole at the top to take the sash-cord. Rope already threaded in and the whole thing lying hidden along the side of the keel, just under the boards. The biggish ones are heavy enough to take a body down to Australia."

"So you reckon we were right not to hold Martin, Mr Masters?"

"I do, Sandy. However we are speculating a bit and I don't

think, sir, there's much more we can do tonight, unless you have any further observations to make."

"None, Judder. These two . . ." he nodded at Finch and Head " . . . are at your complete disposal for as long as it takes. Ashley has his office at Wearbay if you need a base. Now it's up to you."

"Right, sir. We shall start bright and early." He turned to Head. "At what time does the action begin down at the clubhouse in the morning?"

"I'd say at about seven o'clock. I know they serve breakfasts at half-past for those who want them."

"Do they, indeed. If I were there that early, could I join in?"

"I reckon so. For a quid, that is, and as long as you tell them a few minutes before."

"Right. Then here is the plan for tomorrow. We shall all meet at the Wearbay nick at seven o'clock. I take it that from there to the Cullermouth Clubhouse is only a short journey?"

"Three minutes in a car," replied Head.

"Couldn't be better. Now, we need another vehicle. Can you supply one at Wearbay?"

"Easy enough, sir."

"Thank you. Either Tip or Berger will pick it up when we need it. Mr Finch, you will be responsible for the profiles as I have said. I repeat, as fully comprehensive as you can make them, and please ensure that nobody who has been up here leaves Cullermouth without our permission. I want everybody to sail, compete and enjoy themselves as though nothing untoward had happened."

"What about Martin and his boat, sir?" asked Head.

"That will be staying on dry land. He can't sail without a crew, anyway. And the forensic people will want to go over it if they haven't already done so."

"They have," said Pedder.

"With what result?"

"Nothing. I reckon if there was any sort of container used, it will be at the bottom of the North Sea by now."

Masters nodded and then got to his feet. "I think that's all we can usefully do tonight, Mr Pedder, so if you have nothing else for us we'll get off now ready to be up betimes in the morning."

"There's a stock of sandwiches and a drink if you'd like to hang on for a few more minutes."

"We're on," said Green. "I could murder a drink, and a bit of sustenance to carry us over the journey home wouldn't come amiss."

Chapter 2

"JUST A CUP of coffee, please, darling."

"But you can't go thirty or forty miles to Cullermouth without breakfast."

"We shall have a decent breakfast once we get there."

Wanda stood in the kitchen in her dressing gown. "We shall miss you and Bill, you know. It won't be anything like a holiday without you."

"You won't miss us. I want you to come to Wearbay. Later on, of course. In our car. Bring Doris and Michael."

Wanda ran her fingers through her hair. "I don't understand."

"Wearbay is famous for its beaches, and in weather like this, Michael will adore the sand and sea."

"And that's the only reason why you want us there?"

"No. As I understand it, Cullermouth—and by that I mean the sailing club area—will be crawling with wives and children. I don't want you to do anything specific, like asking questions, but I want you to get the feel of the meeting. I want to know whether it's a happy gathering, or whether there are strains that are obviously splitting the crowd. But I don't have to explain. I want an impression which somebody like you can get but I can't. They'll shut up like clams or watch their words if a copper is within earshot, but when you and Doris . . ."

"I won't spy for you, George."

"I've already said I don't want you to ask questions. I want an impression. A total one. And I want it as quickly as possible. We've got to resolve this matter between now and Saturday. I can't hold hundreds of people up here beyond then. They've got work and homes to go to. Quite a lot of them will have to return to their own countries, because

36

this is an international meeting. That limits our time to four days, because we can't count Saturday, the dispersal day."

"I see. But why do you need any impression Doris and I might be able to give you?"

"Because I'm convinced that we'll really have to get under the skin of this one to resolve it. Everybody I've spoken to about Jimmy Cleveland talks of him as an intelligent, even-tempered young man, good at his work and healthy in his pursuits. All of that could be wrong, but just suppose it is right. Why kill him? What rotten cancerous work is going on when a lad can't do a bit of harmless sailing without being poisoned when he's beyond reach of help? So, are his sailing colleagues all pathological specimens? One would say not, otherwise he and other decent boys wouldn't congregate with them. But somebody is. Somebody within that sailing group. And it's on the cards that the other members will have ideas about who is responsible, or someone will have an idea of how it was done, or why. Ideas, I said. Not knowledge or evidence, but feelings. I want you . . ."

She held up her hand, "I think I know what you want. Something intangible but helpful is as near as I can describe it. Something you can't or won't act on, but which might suggest something to you."

"That's it. Now, I'll just finish this coffee and collect Bill who is eating a packet of ginger nuts with his coffee in the sitting room."

"He isn't you know. He's got the biscuits, all right, but he's feeding them to Nel, as well as himself, just outside the front door. He said he was going to wait for the sergeants and the milkman, but I guessed what he was up to, the big softie. He and that dog adore each other."

"I'm pleased to hear it. As long as he doesn't try to kidnap her to take back home."

"What time shall I arrive and where?"

"Try to be at Wearbay police station at about ten. I'll ask somebody there to expect you and to give you directions to the club. One of us will be on the lookout for you at the entrance. Probably Tip."

"Right. And I think I heard your car draw up. Ah, yes, I did. Here's Bill to return the remnants of the packet of biscuits."

"Get me a packet of Bonio or something during the day, love, would you? Nel gets through these so fast I can't keep pace."

"Dog biscuits would be better, William. Ovals, perhaps. Bonios are for taking off and chewing over. You want something you can give Nel two or three of, don't you?"

"You're an understanding lass. Pity we have to go to work today."

"Don't worry, William. George has persuaded me that Doris, Michael and I might like an hour or two on the beach in or near Wearbay."

"Persuaded you?"

"Suggested it might be a good thing on so nice a day. So perhaps I shall see you at lunchtime. If not, be sure we shall have a nice supper ready for you when you come home. And I won't forget that the gin bottle is getting quite low."

"Come on, Bill," urged Masters. "We want to beat the rush hour and get there before breakfast is off."

"I'm with you. Say goodbye to Doris for me, love. See you later."

Masters kissed the end of Wanda's nose and followed the DCI out to the car. As Berger guided the Rover very slowly, with one hand on the wheel, up the narrow, curved slope, he used the other hand to hold up a small paper bag. "For you, Chief."

Masters leant forward to take it. "Thank you. What is it?"

"The newsagent's shop was open early," replied Berger. "I called in for my paper and saw that he sells picture postcards, too. I wasn't intending to buy any, but this one caught my eye. I thought you might like it."

Masters took the card from the bag. It was an aerial view in full colour. He read the legend on the back: 'The Castle and Abbey, Cullermouth, overlooking Abbot's Haven.'

"This is very useful indeed. Take a look, Bill."

What the card showed basically was a headland, almost

38

circular but with a wide neck joining it to the mainland. The cliffs of the headland were precipitous and tumbled, so that the sea was creaming round the rocks at the bottom. Towards the seaward end were scattered ruins of an obviously ecclesiastical nature, the impression being heightened by a graveyard nearby in which, quite plainly, scores of tombstones were still upstanding. The remnants of a wide V-shaped defence wall still stood, incorporating three perfect circles of concrete.

"Old wartime Ack-Ack site," said Green, referring to the circles. "Gun platforms. A lovely spot for them, too."

"Exposed like that?"

"Take another look, chum. At the seaward face of the cliff."

Clear to see, cut in the face were nine or ten huge arches, giving the impression of the peristyle of a cloister.

"There's underground access to that lot," said Green. "I'll bet it was manned by a few platoons of lads on coastal defence. All ready dug for them and safe enough to survive the Hiroshima bomb. I suppose the old Abbots used to walk along there to take the air after compline."

"Maybe so." Masters continued to study the card. Towards the neck of the promontory was the still-standing square keep of a mediaeval castle, with the ruins of walls running from it, without delineating clearly the original shape of the stronghold.

"That must have been a delight to defend," grunted Green. "See, at the landward end, the top of the area is still yards and yards higher than the country round about and on top of that they've built a thumping great defence wall, all nicely angled to give enfilading fire . . ."

"Speak English, please," said Tip.

"Sorry, love."

On either side of the headland were bays with golden yellow sand. That to the north was only a small portion of what Masters supposed must be one of the great beaches of Wearbay. The one to the south was tiny. Cradled between the Castle promontory and a smaller headland—which later he learned was the northern extremity of the river mouth—was the southern bay: a miniature, probably a couple of hundred yards wide at the water's edge. There were three buildings within its arms, for though narrow, it ran back inland for a distance equal to its width. The two buildings under the southern cliffs were hut-like. The one on the northern side suggested a concrete building four-square, on two levels, with a surrounding safety rail.

"That'll be the new clubhouse," said Green.

"I expect you're right. At any rate there are several rows of dinghies parked close by and you can see that a spur road, leading off the main road, has been ramped down in a curve to reach it."

"Very nice," grunted Green. "And that's called Abbot's Haven, is it? Where the old boy used to bring in his Rhenish wine or Malvoisie or whatever his particular tipple happened to be."

"I've no doubt such a spot has seen its fair share of smuggling over the centuries. By the way, Bill, what's that?" Masters put his finger close to the Abbey promontory.

"It's the beginnings of a breakwater," said Green. "Built like a quay, all good and square and solid. That's a crane you can see on it. My guess is it was built to protect the river mouth from erosion and when we see it all, in the flesh, we'll realize it's long enough not only to give that protection, but also to carry the local sewage pipes out to sea and to have a small lighthouse on the end to help commercial shipping coming in and out of the river."

Green sat back to light a cigarette. "Have we been through Durham yet?"

"A while back," said Tip. "I didn't mention it to you because I didn't want to interrupt your conversation with the Chief."

"Quite right, petal. Never butt in . . ."

"*I'm* butting in," said Berger. "There's a tunnel coming up and I shall want you to find the change for the toll."

The run eastwards to the coast was on a broad, uncluttered road that ran straight into Wearbay. A question to an early morning postman got them directions to the police station, and a few minutes before seven they were greeting Ashley Head in his office.

"Nothing new, sir, but I got you this." Head handed over the week's programme of events and sailing instructions. "The names of the committee members are in there, and also all the administrators' names, like Principal Race Officer, Beach Master and so on."

"Thank you. I'll look at it over breakfast. You'll be joining us, I hope."

"Yes, sir. All laid on. They're expecting six of us. Mr Finch will be down there already, I expect."

"Good. Now just one thing. My wife will be calling in here about ten. With Mrs Green and my son. Would you please leave word at your desk that they are to be directed down to the sailing club when they arrive."

"Nothing easier, sir. Your spare car is in the yard when you want it, with local maps."

"Thank you. Now, shall we go? It's a glorious morning and I've a hankering to get down to the water's edge and to have breakfast."

'NO CARS BEYOND THIS POINT. USE ROAD TRAILERS ONLY.'

The notice was displayed where the spur road turned off down to the beach. The local police car drew up and Head came back to speak to Masters. "Do you want to drive down, sir?"

"Not in contravention of the rules," replied Masters. "I've no wish to play the heavy-handed cop. That's a car park I can see on the other side of the road, isn't it?"

"Yes. Pay and display."

"We'll use that."

As they left the car park to walk to the clubhouse, Masters said to Head: "We're going to become part of the scene here. We're going to swamp them with numbers to suck out anything there is to learn. To soak it up if it's there, and to do that properly we are going to have to become honorary members of the club. I see in the programme that by

41

invitation of the Flag Officers and Members of the Cullermouth Sailing Club, all competitors and their crews and various hangers on like wives, children, parents and such like will be honorary members of the club for the King's Cup Week. That's us. As you can see, all my people are in holiday gear. I'd like you to be the same. I should have told you this last night. Perhaps after breakfast you wouldn't mind going off and getting into jeans or slacks or whatever you prefer to wear at the seaside on a day like this."

"Suits me," grinned Head. "Sandals, shorts and a bush shirt is my usual."

"Good. It's a pity about the gent's natty you're sporting at the moment, but the beach would only ruin it, in any case."

The ramp curved downwards until it suddenly petered out in the sand. From that point on, to make it easy for manhandling the road trailers, bands of rubber, half an inch thick and two feet wide, had been laid to take the wheels.

"What are these?" asked Masters. "They're too wide to be old machine belts, I'd have thought."

"Not army beach landing track," said Green. "They use XPM."

"I'm not sure," said Head. "Something similar to this is used both in mining and commercial shipping. Where they wouldn't want to use a metal conveyor belt for fear of causing sparks and such like. The club has obviously been given a load of the worn out stock, because I can see they're using it to make launching points down at the water's edge."

Masters nodded. Two small agricultural tractors had been started up and their drivers were manoeuvring them into some sort of position near the launch sites, presumably for use if something fairly big in the way of boats had to be hauled out of the water.

They stepped up on to the verandah of the clubhouse where the brown bench seats along the wall under the windows, full in the sun, already held a number of people drinking coffee.

They entered a little hallway with a pay phone on the wall, a notice board and signs showing the way to male and female changing rooms, showers, lavatories and drying rooms. Then into the main room which, according to the plate over the door, was known as the Wet Bar.

"What the hell?" demanded Green. "What bar is anything else but wet?"

"The legal bar," said Berger.

"Bar of The House of Commons," added Tip.

"All right, you pair of smarty pants." Green looked about him. "Cor," he murmured. "Concrete floor, no carpet, plastic tables and chairs . . ."

"Now you know why its called the Wet Bar," said Masters. "The sailors can come in here in their wet suits and get a drink as soon as they come ashore. They probably drip all over the floor, that's why there's no carpet or plush upholstery."

"Logical," agreed Green.

Along the back wall was a food counter with an open kitchen behind. Alongside it, closed by a metal grill, was a bar for alcoholic drink. On a long trestle table was an improvised shop selling every type of chocolate bar, crisps, cans of soft drinks, cigarettes, cigars and tobacco, cheap sun hats and other minor items which could conceivably be of use to either the sailors going out to race, or to their families playing on the beaches. A girl of about sixteen was serving a customer— obviously a crew member—with a bottle of suntan oil.

"They'll all need that out on the water in this weather," said Tip. "The sea is so calm it will reflect the sun like a mirror."

"Quite right," agreed Masters. "Especially as even the shorter races last about four hours. That means crews are out for about six hours. Quite a long time to be out in sun as glaring as this."

"Have you ordered breakfast?" A pleasant woman of about thirty-five, wearing a long apron over a summer frock, addressed Tip.

"Yes, I believe we have. For six. There are five of us here already."

"Five. If you'll take a table . . . anywhere."

The red plastic topped tables had been pushed together to form three long rows across the body of the room. They were

43

set with knives and forks. "You can collect what you want from the counter."

"I'd like a pretty big fry-up," said Green.

The woman smiled. "Just ask for what you want. There's sausages, bacon, eggs, tomatoes, chips, toast, margarine and marmalade, with cornflakes to start and either coffee or tea. As much as you want of any or all of them."

"Thanks, love. This is my idea of what a wet bar should be."

"It will be one pound each, please."

"A pleasure. Here's the fiver. But how do you make a profit at these prices?"

She laughed. "We're not out to make a profit." She gestured to the women who, dressed like herself, were busy in the kitchen and at the tables. "We're all members of the club, or wives of the members."

"Nice," replied Green. "Breakfast with love."

"Something of the sort."

They were part way through breakfast before Sandy Finch joined them. A little later another two women appeared carrying large clear plastic bags of bread rolls and huge baps as big as dinner plates, which they put on to a side table. In no time at all they were making all manner of sandwiches from bowls of salad stuffs, sliced meat and pâté.

"That's for the crews to take out, I expect, Chief," said Tip. "Did we know that?"

"You're thinking that young Jimmy could have been fed a poisoned sandwich?"

"It's logical, Chief," said Berger.

"Agreed. Tip, it will be your first job to find out what food Jimmy took out with him."

"You don't sound as if you think a poisoned sandwich could be the answer, Chief."

"I don't, Tip. For one very good reason."

"What's that, sir?" asked Head.

"Timing. Young Jimmy died at half-past-ten. I don't think he would have started to eat his lunch by then, particularly as, in my ignorance, I'm assuming that just before a race and in the early stages is when crews will be most busy and involved in jockeying for position in the fleet. I suspect that it's only after they have shaken themselves out and everything is, literally, more or less plain sailing, that they can get down to eating sandwiches."

"I see what you mean." Tip sounded disappointed.

"Clear the matter up, nevertheless," said Masters. "And while we're at it, I'll give you others some hints of what I would like you to do specifically. Sergeant Berger, did you notice that behind the clubhouse is a high, flat-topped mound?"

"Where all the boats are, Chief?"

"Yes. The dinghy park. The berths are allocated, according to the brochure. They keep the same places all the week. I want you to interest yourself in that. There'll be a lot of to-ing and fro-ing there, especially in the hour before a race and the hour after. There's a road trailer park, too. Combine that in your work."

"Right, Chief."

"Ashley, I believe I saw, near the car park, a camping ground for those competitors who bring caravans or tents. That and the car park is your special area. Tip, apart from Jimmy's food, this place and the women helpers and so on are yours. Bill, upstairs, as I see from the notice near that door in the corner, is the Dry Bar and observation roof and so on. That's your special area of observation. I shall take the water's edge, launching, and so on, together with the Race Office.

"Those are special areas, but please busy yourselves at any time anywhere in the area. We know little of what goes on in such places at times like these. I have a gut feeling that unless we get to know literally everything there is to know we are not going to fathom this business."

Green pushed his plate away. "That feels better," he said. "Now, as I've paid for breakfast, I shall expect somebody to lay on some of the corned beef sandwiches those lasses are making up for my lunch."

"What's your hurry?" asked Tip, who was still eating toast and marmalade.

"I'll tell you, love. Though we know very little about this place, as his nibs has pointed out, it occurred to me that a club of this size must have a full-time steward. If I'm right, and he's the sort of chap he should be, he should know everything there is to know round here. I'm going to find out if I'm right."

Head asked: "Do you want to talk to Harry Martin, Mr Masters?"

"Yes, please. But only after everybody is launched. Then we can have a chat with him in comparative peace, I hope. Will you lay that on, Ashley, as you obviously know him?"

By the time they rose from the table the Wet Bar had begun to fill with a somewhat raucous and definitely mixed crowd. All were wearing their chosen sailing gear. Some—very few—had standard wet suits on, the black rubberized fabric clinging like a second skin to the body. Others had similar wear with short trousers, the length of Bermuda shorts. But for the most part the crews were in a motley regalia of torn nylon overtrousers, patched and repatched, sometimes with one leg torn shorter than the other, and some sort of shirt to keep the sun off the back and shoulders. Without exception the shirts were worn and faded, as indeed were the various items of headgear—linen sun hats, visored scrum caps, wet suit cowls, even an Arab head-dress with spine cloth. On the feet were equally varied items of wear. Wet suit boots, ankle-length and without soles, cut-down gumboots, plimsolls, sandals and, in one case, a pair of pull-on moccasins.

"Hardly a fashion show, is it Chief?" whispered Tip. "That one over there is hardly decent. If he rips that trouser leg much higher he'll be displaying his main halliard."

Masters grinned. "I strongly suspect he's got jockey shorts underneath. I also expect they are as fine a bunch of men as one could find—and I'm not just talking about physique, though there are some pretty good specimens among them."

"All sorts," agreed Tip. "One or two are quite elderly, and I've even seen an oldish woman all togged up and ready to go."

They were, for the most part, drinking coffee from

46

disposable plastic beakers and discussing in noisy groups the placings in the previous day's race which had, apparently, been shortened because lack of wind would not have allowed any craft to sail, in the allotted four hours, the full four rounds of the course, two of which were straight there-and-back legs and two triangular. Obviously some thought that had the second triangle been sailed, they would have caught the leaders; others were discussing a protest concerning some fine point of sailing; and yet more were saying the Race Committee should have moved at least one of the marker buoys to make best use of what little wind did spring up in the early afternoon. As far as Masters could hear, as he moved around, inconspicuously, nobody was discussing the tragic death of Jimmy Cleveland. It was as though everything—venue, weather, company and arrangements—were all combining to make this week so great a success that, temporarily, these people were solely devotees of their sport and not, for the moment, possessed of the ordinary human emotions of inquisitiveness and sadness. Masters guessed this would change as soon as they had dispersed to their normal, everyday lives and occupations. Then the sadness would creep in and maybe last for a long time, particularly if Jimmy had been a popular member of the crowd.

Almost, as if on some sort of signal, the crews started to hurry away. Then almost imperceptibly, the room started to fill with women and children, all dressed for the beach and the sun. The women carried all manner of bags and baskets containing towels, packs of napkins, bathing dresses, plastic rings and balls, buckets and spades, and even knitting.

Tip joined Masters at one of the wide windows overlooking the verandah. The two tractors were now still, but there was other activity on the sand above the water's edge. Four men were talking by the side of a launch marked 'RESCUE'. Two others were loading camera gear on to another marked 'PRESS'. Another pair was putting off in an inflatable to paddle the short distance to a larger motor craft marked 'COMMITTEE' and, forty or fifty yards out, a small catamaran was sailing slowly close to a couple of youths on windsurfers.

47

"Are things beginning to warm up, Chief?"

"I imagine so. The crews, I think, have gone to prepare their craft for the race. I don't know much about dinghy sailing, but one thing I do know, and that is that those who indulge in it spend more time tinkering about with ropes and sheets and sails than they spend on the water. They'll be doing it for the next hour or so, and then they'll start to launch."

"They must like it, Chief."

"Undoubtedly they do, and I'm convinced it is a good, clean, healthy sport, teaching those who indulge in it a great deal of self-reliance, dexterity, weather lore and heaven knows how many other skills."

"Every weekend, apparently. These women must be the equivalent of golf widows, I suppose."

"Not if they and their children can go to the clubhouses and enjoy themselves. Though perhaps we are getting a wrong impression here, where the club is actually built on a beach and we're seeing it in probably the best weather there has been up here for years."

Tip got to her feet. "I think I'll mingle, Chief. The children are beginning to run about outside, now, so the mums will be getting together for a gossip, no doubt. Yes, some are beginning to get cups of coffee. That usually presages a natter."

"Good. I'm going to the Race Office, but I'll be about."

As Masters got to his feet, Berger came in. "Chief, there's a bit of trouble out here in the dinghy park."

"What sort of trouble?" Masters got to his feet to follow the sergeant. "If it's just an argument or local difficulty, it's not our problem. Ashley Head is the one to deal with run-of-the-mill trouble on his own patch."

Berger led the way through a door at the far end of the clubhouse into a narrow passage which turned into a flight of four or five concrete steps leading up to the long tumulus bank which did duty as the dinghy park. "It's about some rope or other that's gone missing, Chief."

"Lifted from one of the boats?"

48

"Apparently."

Masters emerged into the sunlight. "Are there accusations flying about?"

"Not exactly, Chief. Just hard questions being asked. And as the rope is missing from the boat next to Harry Martin's in the line . . . well, you said you wanted everything."

"Quite right. Have you got a list of names matched with allocated berths?"

"The marshal is getting one out for me, Chief. He asked if I could wait until this little lot is out on the water and the panic has died down."

"Right. Where are we?"

Berger stood and pointed along the single line of dinghies, berthed side by side along the mound which, as far as Masters could tell, was a relic of the old defences of the castle which towered above them on its rocky hill. He guessed the mound was not an earthwork in its own right, but the outer bank of a moat which had been dug round the base of the rock to join the sea somewhere near the root of the present pier that carried the harbour light. It was clear that early inhabitants of the castle had ensured that nobody could attack the promontory from any direction without getting his feet wet.

"The one with the blue overall cover is Martin's boat, Chief. It's called *Spearhead*. The forensic boys must have examined it where it is now and then covered it. They roped it down pretty securely."

"I see. And this man who has lost his rope. Who is he?"

"The chap who's pulled his boat forward out of line and tipped it over, Chief. I gathered he had to do that to thread a rope or wire through a block at the top of the mast."

Masters strolled along to the careened dinghy. The name was painted large on the white freeboard of the fibreglass hull—*Slowcoach*.

"Good morning." Masters addressed the man who was reeving a wire through the masthead tackle.

"'Morning." The reply was short. The man was busy. A lean, bespectacled, thirty-year-old in shorts, sandals, and a

49

white T-shirt, with knobbly knees and elbows and a lot of dark hair.

"I don't wish to interfere with your preparations, but would you care to tell me about your missing rope?"

"It's gone. But what business is it of yours?"

"I'm a policeman. I'm interested in things that go missing."

"Well, if you must know, it's a valuable piece of ten millimetre diameter rope. A hell of a long one. The mainsheet, actually."

"Mainsheet? Forgive my ignorance, but I always thought that was the mainsail."

"No. It's the tackle by which the mainsail is trimmed when sailing."

"Tackle? You've lost blocks as well?"

"No. Just the rope. Most people usually mean just the rope itself when they say mainsheet."

"That's what is commonly understood?"

"Yes. Now, if you don't mind, I'd like to get on."

"But without your rope, how can you sail?"

"My crew has gone into the town to get a new one. There's a chandlery van comes down here each day, but not as early as this. It fetches up at the end of the day's sailing, usually, because that's when most replacements are needed. After the day's wear and tear."

"I see. Well, I won't hold you up, but I would like to know if you suspect how the sheet went missing."

"Somebody won it."

"Obviously. But who? Vandals? Kids?"

"Not likely. My boat's cover was on and fastened down. A kid or vandal wouldn't pinch the sheet and then fasten the covers down. They'd more than likely slash the cover to get at what they wanted. If they wanted anything other than to ruin property, that is."

"That's a good observation, sir," said Berger. "So you're pretty certain one of your sailing colleagues borrowed your rope. Perhaps temporarily. Had it got any identifying marks on it?"

"No. It's a sixteen plait, white, soft, strong and flexible.

Thirty feet long. You'll find fifty or sixty like it round here."

"I see. So a search is not likely to help, sir."

"Not a search by you. But I'd recognize it." He stopped work for a moment. "Funny, that, that one should be able to pick out one's own property from among scores of similar ropes, but one gets so used to handling the one item that it becomes familiar."

"Not in the least odd," said Masters. "You'd always know if you were to put on another man's shirt, even though they both came from the same shop and were identical in size, colour, shape and material."

"I suppose so. Now, if you don't mind . . ." He left them abruptly and walked round to the keel side of his tilted craft where something else immediately claimed his attention.

Masters and Berger turned away. "How the hell they manage to sort out that tangle of wire, rope and sails I just don't know. Just look at the number of cleats and pulleys and lord-knows-what screwed on the woodwork. And have you seen the rudders? They're not just straight tillers. They're articulated. To steer one of these you've got to be like a heavy goods vehicle driver."

Masters grinned. "Keep it up. Soak in everything. I have the feeling that unless we get to know all there is to know about sailing, as well as knowing the people, we won't get far on this one."

"You reckon Mr Cleveland and Mr Pedder knew that when they asked for you, Chief?"

"Subconsciously, perhaps. Because this is a bit like one of those locked-room mysteries. Young Jimmy Cleveland was as effectively isolated out there in the dinghy as he would be in that castle dungeon."

"Except that he had Martin with him, Chief."

"I can't believe Martin was involved. For the reasons we've already discussed."

Masters left Berger to continue his prowling round the boat park, and himself returned to the Wet Bar. By this time, many of the dinghies had their sails hoisted, each clearly numbered in heavy black figures two feet high. Though the

51

hulls were of varied colours, most of the sails were white, hanging idly in the still air, held down taut by the weight of the booms.

As Masters entered the clubhouse, Green appeared. "Meet Stan, George. Stan's the steward here. He's going to open the Dry Bar for us, up top."

"Might as well," said Stan. "Too crowded down here, and when the kids get weaving you can't call your soul your own." Masters shook hands. Stan was a big man, late middle-aged and, judging by the tattoos on his arms, an ex-seafaring man, probably from the Royal Navy. He wore old washed out denims and sneakers, a short-sleeved pale blue shirt and a dark blue sleeveless, V-necked pullover. His face was full and weatherbeaten, while the hair had that wispy fawn-grey texture of the former blond.

"The bars will be open as early as this?" queried Masters.

"Club premises," said Stan, "but we've also got a full day licence. Some of those lads like to buy a can of ale to put in the bilges before they go off on days like this. Then there's the visitors. They like the Dry Bar. It's comfy. Armchairs and coffee tables, with a carpet on the floor and pictures on the walls. All boats, of course, but then that's what we're here for."

"You're full-time here, are you?"

"That's right. Busiest on Friday nights, Saturdays and Sundays, of course, but we open Tuesday and Thursday nights, too, in the winter. Every day in summer. Very popular with the crews, this place, and of course we have functions. Even wedding receptions. Helps us keep our heads above water as you might say."

"Good. I expect I'll be seeing you about, Stan."

"I'll be here very hour God sends this week."

"Even better, because I expect you're a chap who keeps his eyes open, so I know Mr Green will want to have a few chats with you about what goes on here. I hope you'll help him where you can."

"I'll do that, sir. I don't like the idea of that young chap getting his. Not that I knew him, mind, except by sight, and not that he was actually killed here in the club, which makes a difference, as you might say."

"In what way, Stan?" asked Green, "He was here for your big week, whether he died within these walls or not."

"It's not the same, snuffing it a couple of miles out to sea."

"You mean distance lends enchantment?"

"I don't know about that, but if somebody's clobbered a couple of miles away from where you live in London you don't feel it the same as if he'd been knocked off on your own doorstep, do you?"

"I suppose not, mate. Though I reckon there must be a flaw in your logic somewhere."

Masters interrupted. "Tell me, Stan, is that why nobody here is talking about Jimmy Cleveland's murder? I know we haven't been here all that long a time, but as far as I know, not one of us has heard it mentioned. Frankly, I'd have expected it to be a bit of a nine days' wonder, but apparently I'm wrong."

Stan scratched his head. "You said murder, sir. Nobody here reckons it is. What I mean is they know you lot think it is, but they think different. So they're treating it different. And as I say, it was two miles out, not near anybody but Harry Martin who was in the boat with him, and the meeting's going on as if nothing had happened. And then there's the wives and kids around, it's lovely weather, and they're all here enjoying themselves no end. No, sir, everything's wrong for it to be murder. So they don't talk about it—not in the way you mean, at any rate."

"The wrong atmosphere for murder, is it?" asked Green.

"That's right. So I don't reckon you detectives are going to get anywhere, but you want to enjoy yourselves while you're here. No point in wasting your time altogether."

Masters laughed. "Thanks for the encouragement, Stan. I'll leave you now, but I'd like you to tell Mr Green everything you can about overnight security of the dinghies berthed outside. He'll question you pretty closely, so have it all ready."

When Masters reached the Wet Bar, Ashley Head was waiting for him. Head was now in shorts, sandals, T-shirt, and a white, floppy sunhat, the brim of which was close-stitched and lined with green.

"I've laid on Harry Martin for half-past-ten, sir. Where will you see him?"

"What about upstairs in the Dry Bar? There's likely to be a bit of privacy up there."

"His wife's up here with him. They're staying in a small hotel in Wearbay."

"Right. If she comes in with him, I'll see them both together. I'd like you there, too. And Tip. Nothing formal."

Head grinned. "Dressed like this, Chief? It wouldn't be very easy to be formal."

Masters shook his head. "Don't you believe it, Ashley. You don't have to lose dignity, personality or formality if you're dressed in nothing more than a towel. Chaps like generals were dressed like gypsies in the desert campaigns on occasions, but they maintained their aura."

Head looked solemn. "Come to think of it, Chief, Gandhi used to wear only a loincloth and he kept his dignity, I seem to remember."

"It's a point worth remembering. Clothes don't necessarily make the man. Now, what about your area of operations?"

"The camp site? I'm just going there. I had to rush home to change and see Martin . . ."

"Of course. But get there before everybody leaves the site, otherwise you'll have no joy."

Head went off and Masters again took his seat in one of the large picture windows of the Wet Bar. From this vantage point he could see all that went on in the little bay and hear and see everything in the clubhouse.

Tip joined him. "Nobody's talking, Chief. At least, not about the murder. There's enough chatter about everything else, but I've not heard Jimmy Cleveland's death mentioned once."

"They are not ganging up on you?"

"No. Nothing like that. There are no awkward silences when I approach and they all say hello and smile. Genuinely, I mean. I just don't think this murder means anything to

54

them, or rather they've pushed it to the back of their minds because otherwise it might be uncomfortable."

"There may be something in what you say, Tip. So make use of their attitude. They're prepared to be friendly. Meet them half way. Sooner or later you'll either hear something or be able to steer conversations your way."

"In other words, Chief, I'm to act as if I was one of them—a wife or girlfriend of one of the sailors."

"Exactly. Join in and mix. It will probably be easier for you when Wanda and Doris Green arrive. You'll be a group within the party."

They sat silent, watching the activity in the clubhouse. It was incessant. Helms and crews were coming in to pick up packed lunches and cans of coke or lager. A number bought Mars bars and chocolate wafers. The women making the sandwiches were still beavering away, cutting baps, buttering, making up, wrapping up in clingfilm and selling, all at the same time. A few people were still at the tables, drinking coffee, while the children had started to roar around, whooping and calling, screaming and shouting.

"It's bedlam, isn't it?" said a pleasant-faced young woman passing close to them. She had a bunch of keys on her apron belt. She used them to unlock a large chest freezer situated against the wall between the windows. As she opened the lid she added, "I've heard more noise in here since last Saturday than you get in any school playground." She lifted out of the freezer a clear plastic sack full of pale-looking sausages. Masters got quickly to his feet to help her. "Thanks," she said. "There's twenty-eight pounds in there. Just hang on to them would you a moment, while I find some beefburgers . . . ah, here we are. Five pounds. That should be enough for the little horrors."

"These are for the children?"

"There'll be two or three dozen of them here for lunch."

"And their mothers and guests and workers both in here and outside?"

"That's right. Now, chips. Better have a full bag . . . no, two. Twenty pounds."

55

"Any peas?" asked Masters, peering into the depths of the chest.

"Not today. We're giving them baked beans. And the yoghurts are being delivered by the dairy van. So that's it." She closed the freezer with a soft thud and relocked it.

"You keep it locked?"

"All the time."

"Against pilfering?"

"I don't know, as I've never lost anything, but I'm taking no chances. One of these little perishers could open the lid and leave it open and I'd lose all the stock."

"Of course. But they could also either switch off at the power point or pull out the plug."

She looked up at Masters. "Do you know, I hadn't thought of that. I'll have to lay on hourly inspections. This is the first time our club has hosted an important meeting like this and, quite frankly, we don't know the drill."

"You appear to be doing very nicely."

"Oh, we can do as well as anybody when it comes to hospitality. All our volunteers are good housewives. They can cope very well indeed, but it's the little things that you can only learn by experience. For instance, nobody can phone out because we didn't ask British Telecom to empty the coin box last week . . . oh, and lots of other little things like that."

"Never mind. Now, where would you like these sausages? Am I allowed to carry them through into your kitchen for you?"

"Yes, please."

"In that case I'll take a bag of chips, too. That will just leave you one bag of chips and the beefburgers."

"Cold to the hands, aren't they?" she commented as she led the way out of the end door and down the passage towards the showers before turning off through another door into the large, open kitchen.

She hoisted her bags on to the central table. "Lucy," she called to another woman of about her own age. "You're supervising lunches, aren't you?"

"For the kids? Yes."

"Not for the adults, too?"

"No, Gloria's doing that. Bangers, she said."

"Right. Here are your burgers and chips. When the yoghurts come, would you see he doesn't leave them outside in the passage, or lots of little fingers will be helping themselves."

"I'll get him to put them in the stockroom."

"Can I put these on the table, too?" asked Masters.

"Oh, yes, of course. I should have asked you . . . here, would you like to dribble your hands under the hot tap to warm them up? Lucy, is there a clean hand-towel?"

"Please don't bother," said Masters. "I can easily . . ."

"Here," interrupted Lucy, holding out a large mug of steaming coffee. "Put your hands round that. It'll soon warm them up."

Masters didn't want the coffee, particularly, but in offering it, Lucy had provided him with a ready-made excuse to linger in the kitchen, in among these women who, he guessed, were intelligent and normally inquisitive, seeing most of what went on in the clubhouse. They could become a good source of information: at least it was worthwhile becoming accepted by them.

Lucy perched on the table, clasping her own mug of coffee. "What do you sail?" she asked Masters.

"I don't sail at all." Secretly he was a little surprised that this woman did not realise who and what he was.

"I wouldn't have thought sailing was a spectator sport," she said. "But when you count up the number of people here who are neither helms nor crews one begins to wonder. I know I've spent many a miserable, cold Sunday sitting in a clubhouse while my old man spent the time out on the water. Out of sight, too. We must be crackers to marry dinghy sailors." She turned as the first woman approached. "Liz, there's coffee in the pot. The real thing. I've given Mr . . . er . . . your friend some, but there's plenty left."

"Ta! But I would hardly call this gentleman my friend though, come to think of it, he knocks spots off my old man when it comes to physique, so I'll change that answer. My new-found friend, Mr . . . er . . .?"

"Masters."

"Don't tell me. You've got a wife just outside the kitchen. Not that young woman you were sitting with, she wasn't wearing any rings . . ."

"That young lady," replied Masters, "is a member of my staff."

"I see. What staff is that? Are you press or a marine photographer or something like that, Mr Masters?"

"I'm a policeman."

"A policeman? You? Sent here to see nobody half-inches our spoons?"

"Don't be silly, Liz," said Lucy, over the rim of her cup.

Liz gazed at her for a moment and then the penny dropped. "Oh! You're here because of Jimmy Cleveland, I suppose?"

"That's right."

"I suppose you have to look into all sudden . . . wait a moment. Did you say Masters?"

"Yes."

"That name rings a bell." Liz put her mug on the table. "Didn't I read about a big noise from Scotland Yard . . . that's right. Last year. You solved all those murders in Nortown. You remember, Lucy. That man who killed a woman every month when the moon was full, or something like that."

Lucy looked at Masters. "Jimmy Cleveland only died yesterday morning," she said quietly. "And they've got a Scotland Yard detective up here already? That means . . ."

"It means as much or as little as you care to read into it," replied Masters. "I'm on holiday up here with my wife and young son. We are staying in a cottage at Stannup with one of my colleagues and his wife. We were asked to . . . well, to look into things by the boy's father. He's a senior policeman, you know."

"Yes, I knew that. I'd met Jimmy Cleveland several times. He often sailed up here at one time. When he was quite a boy and before he moved south. But you said that girl out there was one of your staff. So you've got more people here than just you and your married colleague."

"Yes. That young lady is Woman Detective Sergeant Tippen. She and a male colleague drove up here yesterday evening."

"Oh, lor!" moaned Lucy. "So it definitely is murder, you think?"

"I'm afraid so."

"I'd heard a rumour that it was murder, but all the men pooh-poohed it, so I disregarded the rumour."

"Have you arrested Harry Martin, Mr Masters?" asked Liz.

"No. Should I have done?"

"Well, if it was murder, the only possible person who could have killed Jimmy Cleveland was the only other man in the boat with him. Even I can see that, though anybody who thinks Harry Martin would murder his crew is daft. And you say you haven't arrested Harry."

"That's true."

"Then it can't be murder, can it? Or you can't be sure it is, I mean, because you don't let the only possible guilty person remain at large if you are sure, do you?"

Masters grinned. "There's a great deal of impeccable logic in what you say, but your reasoning is a little less than sure, shall we say. But you're right. I try never to arrest anybody unless I am a hundred per cent certain, in my own mind, of his guilt."

"And you have no evidence against Harry Martin?"

"I haven't even looked for any."

"You're a funny policeman," said Lucy.

"Many people have accused me of being far worse than funny."

"I can imagine. But what do you think of Harry Martin? We all like him up here."

"I haven't even met him," said Masters offhandedly. "I'm going to, of course. I think he's coming down to see me after this morning's launch. I shall probably have a chat with him and Mrs Martin, if they come together, as I hope they will."

"Excuse me," said Liz, "but there's a rather stunning woman signalling this way . . ."

Masters turned. "Ah, yes, my wife. She's brought our boy down to see the sea. Thank you for the coffee, ladies. No doubt I shall see you about."

"I've no doubt he will, either," said Lucy when Masters was out of earshot.

"Don't let that one fool you, Liz. He's not quite as harmless as he sounds and looks."

"I wouldn't mind the chance of finding out," said Liz with a grin.

"With opposition like that?" asked Lucy, staring as Masters reached Wanda and kissed her lightly.

"Now you're spoiling it," moaned Liz.

"She's good-looking," said Lucy firmly. "And I mean good-looking, not beautiful or pretty or anything like that. And she's got a smashing figure and she's beautifully groomed. What chance do we stand against opposition like that when all we're doing here is frying bangers and chips?"

Liz shrugged her shoulders. "It would be a bit of a challenge, wouldn't it? To try, I mean."

Lucy said: "If that's how you feel. But I've never known you to look at another man. Ted has always been good enough for you up to now."

"And still is, silly. I just thought, just for a moment, how nice it would be . . ."

Lucy jumped down from her perch on the table. "I know exactly what you mean. But you're thirty-five, not sweet sixteen."

"I know. Still . . . I wonder if he'll be coming to the barbecue tonight?"

"Why?"

"It just occurred to me that if they have a little boy, mum might just have to stay at home to babysit."

"You're heading for trouble, my girl. Particularly with that one."

"He's from London. That's different from somebody who lives locally."

"Well, don't say I didn't warn you—if you do go ahead with it, at all. Now, where are these perishing beefburgers?"

"Darling," said Wanda, "we got here very early, so I've left Michael with Doris on the beach just round the corner of the headland. There's miles of beautiful sand there. Nicer than in this little bay. Over there it's golden. Here it's a bit grey-looking."

"Very definitely not so nice here, because it is churned up so often by tractors and launching trolleys and it gets a deal of litter left lying about, I imagine. And talking of launching trolleys, the dinghies are beginning to go into the water. Come outside and watch."

They found Tip on the verandah. Masters left the two women and strolled to the end of the concrete. He saw that at the seaward end of the clubhouse a ramp had been built of old sleepers: a slipway down from the raised bank of the dinghy park to the level of the sand. More of the wide, heavy rubber strips had been laid from the bottom of the ramp across the end of the clubhouse and out towards the middle of the little bay where spurs of the same material, set at right angles, ran down to the edge of the gently lapping water. At the top of the ramp, on each side, were two ropes, obviously there to help haul the boats back up to their berths. Nobody was using them to steady the boats coming down. The helm and crew member of each team were taking hold of the side handles of the launching trolleys at the bow end and, leaning back against the momentum of their craft on the slope, were easing them gently down, soles slipping slightly on the finely powdered sand that covered the rubber underfoot.

"I didn't know they put the sails up before they launched," said Wanda joining him. "I had visions of them hauling up when they were afloat."

"I suppose it can be done either way, but as they all seem to be doing the same thing it is probably easier to do on dry land or when moored."

"Or alongside a jetty," suggested Tip.

61

"Could be."

The first three or four boats were floated off the trolleys which were wheeled stern first into the water until the hulls lifted. Then the helms climbed aboard, wet up to their backsides, while their crews pulled the trailers back on to the beach where a band of six or seven youths took over to haul the little vehicles a dozen or so yards back from the water's edge where they were parked neatly, ready to be used at the end of the race.

"They've got it well laid-on," said Tip, noticing this. "I wonder who or what the boys are?"

They were obviously in charge of a small, deep-tanned man of about forty who was, at a guess, the Beach Master. "I'll try and have a word with him later," announced Tip. "He can probably tell me exactly what happened when Harry Martin's boat returned yesterday."

"Get full details," said Masters.

"Yes, Chief. Have you examined the boat yet?"

"Not yet. I'm going to let the fun and games die down first."

"I think I'll mingle a bit, Chief. See what the next scene is likely to be."

"I'll come, too, if I may," said Wanda. "I would like a cup of coffee if such a thing is available."

"Nothing easier," said Tip. "The place is awash with it."

After leaving Masters, Ashley Head had made his way up the slope and out of the bay of Abbot's Haven, to cross the road and enter the car park. The car-standing area was long and narrow, bounded by chain-link fencing with a few trees on the south side and a continuous hedge of bushes and trees on the north. These separated the camp site from the car park. The site itself was the continuation of the moat part of the rampart which formed the dinghy park. Head could see several caravans and a number of tents pitched there, but to get to them he had to go to the end of the car park and then turn right and right again. Then he was walking on the grassy bottom of this artificial valley which appeared wide enough

62

to take quite large tents on both sides of its central track.

The Cullermouth Club had negotiated with the local council for the use of this area. At meetings such as this, attracting large numbers of people, a significant number were students or young people as yet earning insufficient money to pay expensive hotel bills. Cullermouth, unlike some clubs which had spartan dormitories for housing such members, had been obliged to make provision for these people otherwise they would not have been considered as the host club. The local council, only too happy to encourage a large number of visitors to stay for a week—and thus to spend money—within their boundaries, had been pleased to make this area available, and had put up a stand pipe for water. As the car park already boasted adequate lavatories, the site was ideal for this one-off week of use as the sailors' camp. Head noted how clean and peaceful it was and hoped that he would not find it totally deserted.

He needn't have bothered. First off he heard a radio playing quietly and then a female voice asked courteously enough, "Excuse me, but are you a resident of this site?"

Head turned to face the woman who had spoken from the doorway of a tent.

"No. My name is Head. I'm a policeman and I'd like . . ."

"In those clothes? A policeman? You'd better not go on point duty in Newcastle in those trousers." Head remembered what Masters had said about maintaining one's dignity dressed only in a towel. The thought caused him to smile, and the smile turned to a laugh. The woman thought this was in appreciation of her joke. She was wrong. Head was laughing at himself because, for the first time in his life as a policeman, he found himself smiling and approaching a serious-case interview with anything but a cold, austere or even bad-tempered attitude. And this pleased him. He liked the thought.

"They are a bit like tinker's mufti, I must admit. But they're just the job for weather like this."

"Well, you've got the legs for them. Not all thin and pale and white. Good, solid, dark and hairy."

63

"Thank you." He put his hand into the hip pocket of his shorts and brought out his wallet. "My identification, ma'am."

"How lovely. I've never been shown a policeman's ID before, and I love being called ma'am. Makes me feel like the Queen."

"You're not supposed to say that. You're supposed to ask me my business."

"I see. So what can I do for you?"

"Chat for a bit."

"Well, I must say, that's a new approach."

"You and anybody else left on the camp site."

"Now you've spoiled it. Just when I was about to invite you in." She laughed. "There are three or four of us about. Shall I try to round them up?"

"If you wouldn't mind."

Soon Head found himself sitting in a caravan with four women and a baby. It was close quarters—an intimate party—which, he realised, was totally unlike the ambience of any police interview he had ever conducted before. He began to marvel at the way Masters could change the way a detective's mind worked. Like all his colleagues in the NEC, he had not forgotten how Masters had fathomed a multi-murder mystery, which had had them baffled for a year, by theories and practice which they had regarded as whimsical rubbish—until it had proved him right.

"You'll know it's about Jimmy Cleveland," said Head to his eager listeners. "He was poisoned out at sea . . ."

"How do you know that?"

"That he was poisoned?"

"No. That he was poisoned out at sea? Couldn't he have been poisoned on land? Something he ate for breakfast, perhaps?"

"No good, I'm afraid," said Head. "The poison in his innards was the sort of stuff that works immediately. Inside a minute, sometimes."

"Something he ate or drank while at sea, then?"

"That's a possibility, but we think not. Harry Martin says he didn't have anything."

"My old man," said the woman with the baby, "takes garlic perles every morning."

"Pearls?"

"P-E-R-L-E-S," she spelt out. "They're supposed to be good for the circulation or something."

One of the others laughed. "Looking at what you've got on your lap, Tina, I should say they're good for both circulation *and* something, not *or* something."

"What? Oh, I see. Yes. Well, the point is, Hilary's perles are those little gelatine capsules. Slow-release, I think they're called. If somebody took poison in those it would be quite a long time before it acted."

"Point taken, love," said Head. "But that raises one or two points. First, those gelatine capsules only hold up release for about twenty minutes after the stomach acids get at them, and Cleveland had been out on the water for an hour and a half when he collapsed. Second, he wasn't taking any sort of pill for anything, so he wasn't likely just to swallow one for no reason. Third, you said, 'if somebody took poison in one of those . . .'. That suggests Jimmy Cleveland committed suicide. And we're pretty certain he didn't. So it's not a question of whether he took poison so much as being given poison. Do you get me?"

"I get you," said Tina. "You reckon somebody administered it to him. That points to Harry Martin."

"Who we don't think would kill his crew, and we have strong reasons for believing he didn't."

"I must admit," said another woman, whom Head had heard addressed as Jenny, "that I can't see Harry Martin murdering anybody. He's a lamb. A real one, I mean, not a wolf in lamb's clothing."

"That squares with what everybody says about him," agreed Head, "but we have to keep a bit of scepticism about that, because we don't reckon anybody can tell who will or will not kill somebody else, given what they consider to be a good reason."

"People do funny things." She turned to the camper Head had met first. "Remember that chap Tully, Clare? He nearly killed a chap who asked him to have a drink."

"I remember," said Clare. "I was really frightened at the time."

"What happened?" asked Head.

"Tully was TT and a religious maniac," said Jenny. "One of those thin, nervous types. This other man, who didn't know him, got talking to him in our clubhouse one day and after a few minutes invited him to have a drink. Tully went berserk. Accused this man of mocking him, trying to corrupt the believers and generally belonging to the hosts of Satan. When the other chap tried to protest that he'd been misunderstood, Tully hit him. And that led to a right old set to. The men who pulled them apart said Tully had the strength of a maniac and could well have killed the other man."

"There you are, then," said Head. "So, ladies, we're looking about us. We don't expect anybody to point a finger and say 'that's the murderer', but we do want to know any gossip."

"Concerning Jimmy Cleveland?" asked Mary, the fourth woman.

"Not specifically him."

"I was going to say you wouldn't hear much. Jimmy wasn't one to cause gossip, if you know what I mean. He didn't run after other men's wives or girlfriends, and he was always cheerful and open." She turned to the others. "Wouldn't you have said so?"

They all nodded. Clare added: "And Harry Martin's the same. He's married, of course, but he's devoted to Mandy, and I'm sure she and Jimmy Cleveland weren't playing Harry up."

"You're sure?" queried Head.

"Absolutely. Jimmy has his own boat, you know. He's not sailing it here, in the King's Cup, because it's a bit old and slow for this sort of company, but he sails it all the time down south, and his girlfriend, Janet, crews for him. He agreed to crew for Harry when he was asked, otherwise he wouldn't have been involved in this meeting. So, you see, Jimmy and

Mandy Martin hardly ever met, except perhaps just now and again in the clubhouse."

"Thank you. Just one question about that. Who usually crews for Martin?"

"Barry Duke. He's a school teacher. He just couldn't get off in term time to come up here."

Head nodded. "Is Duke married?"

"No."

"Girlfriend?"

"Nobody specific."

"Young Cleveland didn't by any chance pinch this Janet girl from him?"

Clare said, "Just a moment! What are you getting at? Trying to accuse Barry Duke of killing Jimmy out of jealousy over Janet?"

"Just the opposite," said Head blandly. "I'm trying to eliminate him. Be fair, ladies, you know we have to think of everybody and everything. Then we try to rule out whatever we can, and whoever. Just because we ask a question about somebody you know it doesn't mean we're accusing them of murder or even seriously considering them."

"In that case, why ask?"

"Because if you told me that this girl, Janet, and Barry Duke had at one time been pretty thick, I'd have wanted to ask both of them what had caused the split, just to make sure Jimmy Cleveland hadn't put Barry Duke's back up to a point where there was bad blood between them."

"That seems fair enough," said Tina. "Would somebody hold the baby for a moment while I make coffee?"

"Put him in his cot," said Jenny.

"I can't at the moment. I've put all the cot clothes out to get a blow in the fresh air and I'm not going to bring them in for a bit yet."

"Give him to me," said Mary. "Here, come on, Goliath. Have a change of laps."

Head waited until this little interruption was over, and then said, "Because there is a bit of hanky-panky going on

67

between some of the members of the Association, isn't there?"

"How do you know?"

"Officially it's called information received. Here and now I'd prefer to say a little birdie told us. Well, not so little actually, or do I mean not so much of a birdie as an old rooster? Anyhow . . ."

He paused while the girls laughed.

"Anyhow, that apart, I don't reckon there could be a big gathering of men and women, like this, where about a couple of hundred of you are swanning about in each other's company, miles from home, for a week, without there being a bit of hanky-panky, could there? My experience tells me it would be an impossibility."

"Is that why you came to the camp site?" asked Clare, coldly.

"I don't follow you, love."

"Don't 'love' me," she spat at him. "That old cat Vera Bartram has been spreading her poison again, hasn't she? About me. That's why you're here. Coming to the site, all friendly and matey, dressed up like a beachcombing yob to worm your way into our confidence and nose out all the dirt."

Head looked taken aback. Or at least he hoped he did. Masters had said play it softly, play it cannily. Was this the moment to withdraw? He quickly decided it was. After an attempt at a repair job.

"Actually," he said, "I'm not at liberty to say whether it was or wasn't Vera Bartram who gave us our information, but one thing I can tell you, and that is that the name of Clare Somebody-or-other has never been mentioned to me or to any of my colleagues as far as I know." He got to his feet, remembering that this was to be a dignified retreat. "I hadn't meant to question any of you ladies about your personal lives, and so I'll go now."

"You said gossip," said Jenny.

"Certainly I did. But I meant . . . oh, I don't really know what I did mean, because until we hear what it is we want to know, we shan't be able to judge what's useful and what isn't.

Probably I meant to ask for your opinions rather than gossip, but we really do want to know what members think about Jimmy Cleveland's death, or whether anybody has seen anything strange happening here, in the camp, or in the car park."

"Strangers, you mean?"

"If there have been any, yes. Or if you've seen somebody trying to dispose of something surreptitiously, or messing about with the boats."

"Why didn't you say all this earlier?" demanded Mary.

"Because I didn't want to subject all you ladies to police interviews. I thought a friendly chat would be more acceptable to you and a hell of a lot nicer for me. I'm just sorry that Clare jumped to the conclusion I was prying into some private affair of hers. I don't know what she's referring to, of course, and I shan't ask her. All I would ask you ladies to do is to accept my apology for upsetting Clare and—if you wouldn't mind—to let me know if you see, hear or think of something that could be of use to us. Anything, however small."

"Stay for coffee," said Tina. "It's made."

"I'd better not, but thanks all the same. I've obviously spoilt Clare's morning for her already."

Stooping to avoid hitting his head on the door lintel, Head left the caravan. He forced himself to walk slowly away. But once he was out of sight of the four women, he hurried to find Masters. Maybe what he had got would be of no value, but at least it was a chink in the armour of these people who had put on the chain-mail of indifference to the unresolved death among their number. Besides, Matt Cleveland was his boss, and oddly enough he had a great deal of time for the DCS whose man-management was based on friendliness rather than heavy discipline.

"Nice place you've got up here, Stan," said Green, surveying the Dry Bar.

"Not bad, is it. Mark you, this is the show-place. Where we

69

hold all our wedding receptions, parties, meetings and so on."

"Just the place for . . . what's the equivalent term in the boating world for *après-ski*?"

"I know what you mean. The only drawback from my point of view is them windows." Stan pointed to the huge picture windows on the sea end and the bay frontage of the room.

"Useful for watching the boats."

"Mebbe, but I 'as to clean 'em. There's enough glass there to cover a tennis court, an' being so near the sea they gets covered in salt. You can scrape the rime off those like heavy frost in the winter. An' being outside up a ladder sloshing water about is no joke with some of the winds we get up here. An' the cost of the curtains! Something stinking, the price was. They're long, you see and have those rope-pulls to open an' close them. I tell you what, Mr Green, I asked the committee to let us have them down in the summer because the sun rots and fades them so much you wouldn't believe it. But would they let me do it? No, Stan, they said, it would spoil the look of the room. And it'll spoil the look of the bank balance in a couple of years' time if I don't, I said. But there was no shifting them."

"Nice seats and chairs," said Green.

All round the two walls under the windows were leather-look sofas in Burgundy red. Each sofa was fronted by a coffee table and two matching armchairs on the other side of it. At two points, backing pillars between the windows, were writing tables and chairs. In the main body of the room, comfortable looking fireside chairs were grouped in families around more coffee tables. The bar took up half the long wall opposite the windows. The other half was occupied by a pool table, and doors to lavatories. The landward short end had a darts board and a wide, double door to an open-air observation plaform, from which ran a flight of steps up to the flat roof of the Dry Bar, again an observation platform guarded by railings, but also supporting two flagstaffs with jack-stays.

"Not bad," grunted Green. "Not bad at all. And it's a nice

drop of carpet you've got here. Wall-to-wall. This must have cost the club a bomb."

"Ah!" said Stan.

"Ah, what?" enquired Green.

"There's ways an' means," said Stan. "In a set-up like this there's always a member who can get what you want at the right price, if you know what I mean."

"Why not?"

"Why not? They pretend they're doing you a favour. They're not. It's what's known as PR. They supply something like this carpet at cost or a bit over and then do thousands of pounds' worth of business because of it."

"It's what's known as casting your bread upon the waters," said Green.

"I know that one. An' it'll come back a hundred-fold. But when there's two who want to cast the same bit of bread, who gets what comes back can cause a raft of trouble."

Green whistled silently. "You mean two members wanted the bunce?"

Stan unlocked the door of the bar and went behind the counter to lift the security grill. "And the rest," he added.

Green leant beside the beer handles. "Are you going to tell me?"

"Nothing to tell, really, except that one's in a big way of business and the other isn't. So Mr Big can get the carpet out of the makers cheaper and quicker."

"Because his orders are bigger and his credit's better?"

"That's right. An' his car's bigger and his house is bigger an' so's his wife, while Mr Little has a secondhand car, a little house and a little cracker of a wife—when it comes to looks, I mean."

"I think I get you," said Green. "Little Mrs Little likes what Mr Big's got and Mr Big is not all that averse to her interest, while Mrs Big and Mr Little don't like it at all."

"You've got it mate. Now, what'll you have?"

"A drop of your ale. It's good up here."

"None better. Here, try that for size."

Green gulped a couple of inches from the top of the glass.

71

"Trouble, was there?"

"Still is."

"Going to tell me about it?"

"I've told you enough. I'd lose my job if I named names and somebody got to know or even suspected I had."

"Fair enough," said Green. "How much do I owe you?"

"On me. I'll have one with you later."

They were still chatting when a young man arrived. "I'm not late, am I Stan?"

"No, well on time, Sam. I just thought I'd open up for you. This here's Mr Green, a detective from Scotland Yard."

"Hello. Are you on duty, or . . ."

"Would I say I was with a glass of beer in my hand?"

"Sam's here to take over the bar for a couple of hours," said Stan. "The members do it in turns. Saves money on paying temporary staff at race meetings like these."

"Good wheeze," said Green, "but it doesn't look as though you're going to be very busy, Sam."

"He will be," said Stan. "After about eleven."

"I've brought some reading I want to do," said Sam, "so I'm not worried."

Green put down his empty glass and strolled across to one of the panorama windows. "They're getting into the water," he said. "In fact some of them are quite a way out. It looks like slow going to me."

"It will be in this weather, but they'll catch a drop more wind once they're clear of the headland."

Green turned. "I'd best see what the rest of my crowd is doing. See you about, Stan. Cheers, Sam."

The Principal Committee vessel and the Assistant Committee vessel, both heavy boats with inboard motors, were already speeding out to the course which, because it was north of the river entrance, could not be seen from the Haven, the view that way being obstructed by the long quay of the lighthouse. The marine photographer, in his outboard craft, was moving just offshore, with only enough way on his boat to keep it under control. His job—and hence his livelihood—depended on him being where the boats and crews were at all times. Photographs are sold to people, and people like to see themselves in a photograph before they buy. The sailing correspondent had not yet asked for his craft to be put in the water. His main interest was in results. The few inches of copy he was normally allowed above the listed results would take him no time to write, especially as there were certain items which always had to be mentioned— the weather being the most important, with references to foreign competitors coming second.

Masters and Wanda strolled across the soft, dust-dry sand to the point where they could watch the activity at the launching spurs. "It seems to me," said Wanda, "that they can never put everything they have to have into the boat before it is launched. Just look at them. They float the boats off the trolleys, but they don't move away to make room for somebody else to follow them. No, they have to hold them there while somebody fetches something that has been forgotten. There, see? That one's putting a rudder on board. Here comes another with a pack of sandwiches and a thermos. And look at that chap. He's got a rope caught up in something. He'll have his boat over if he doesn't sit down."

Masters grinned down at her. "I suspect they know exactly what they're about, poppet. Orderly chaos is what they like and that's what they achieve."

The sails hung limp on the masts of the dinghies already afloat, waiting for their helmsmen to take control of the booms and bring their heads on to the tacking course to get out to sea. But there seemed to be no urgency until the Beach Master started to use his megaphone to transmit requests to craft to get going. Slowly, almost sluggishly, the craft started answering to their helms. The merest of breezes wiggled the sails and then bellied them slightly, so that the craft seemed to spurt for a yard or two before settling back to a sedate pace which caused no more than ripples at bow and stern. The sun caused shadows: elegant craft darkening the water with shimmering blobs of darkness, in no way reflecting the image of the boats themselves. Almost imperceptibly they clawed their way out, some tacking far over to the south before coming about, others making smaller zigzags on either side of a straight line to the mouth of the cove.

"Leisurely and peaceful, isn't it?" murmured Wanda.

"Meaning murder is out of place?"

"I suppose it was murder?"

"Alf Pedder thinks so."

"Do you?"

"I find it hard to believe that a young man could be so painfully poisoned, two miles out to sea, by accident."

"Painfully?"

"Agonizing and rapid. Accident is out because there is no reason why anybody should use cyanide for anything these days, let alone in sailing a dinghy. The stuff is not easily obtainable, either, so it means that there was an effort made to get it and then to carry it out to sea. The only alternative to murder, therefore, is suicide."

"Which you rule out?"

"I wouldn't rule it out if cyanide were easily obtainable or if it didn't cause so horrible a death. No bright young man as Jimmy Cleveland is reported to have been would go to those lengths to commit suicide these days, when all one has to do is to take enough tablets with a few large drinks . . . no, darling, it's all wrong. He was up here to enjoy himself. He was actually having fun, so the place and time is wrong for suicide. And then, his life. A new job, a new flat, a new boat, a new girlfriend. They all argue against him having been reduced to a state in which he might contemplate taking his own life."

"So you are convinced it is murder."

"I'm afraid so, my sweet. And quite frankly, I'm foundering."

"Darling," expostulated Wanda, "you only heard of the tragedy last night, and you've been on the job less than three hours."

"I know. But I usually have some idea of what I'm about. Here it would be easy to arrest Harry Martin and say he must be the murderer because he was the only one anywhere near

74

young Cleveland at the time. But I cannot accept that for a good many reasons which seem valid enough to me, at any rate."

"Something must have held back Mr Pedder and the local police from arresting him, too."

"Just so. And you would think it would be the easiest thing in the world to do. But like me, they would want something other than propinquity as a basis for arrest. One must ask whether young Cleveland would have died had he crewed in another boat, or alternatively, if some other chap had crewed for Martin, would he have died in Jimmy's place? And that's not all. There are various other possibilities."

"So what are you doing about them?"

"The only thing I can do. Put out feelers. Spread the team around all the different areas of activity here and try to prod some hint out of them. But I must admit I've been surprised by what I've found down here."

"It is a bit of an eye-opener. Everything is so well laid on in such a friendly way."

"It isn't that which has surprised me. It is the absolute lack of interest in Jimmy's death. I imagined, in my innocence, that the place would be buzzing with talk about it. After all it only happened yesterday morning. But no! When we arrived this morning, there was no talk about it, nor has there been since, as far as I can make out."

"They probably wouldn't like talking in front of policemen."

"This lot? These are your middle-class law and order buffs. Professional men and women who, if we are to believe what we are told, would jump at the chance of helping the police. Actively, I mean. Yet you are suggesting they are watching their tongues just because we are here. They're not watching their tongues, poppet. They're just not talking about Jimmy's death at all."

"A conspiracy of silence?"

"I wouldn't have thought so. They're chattering about everything else under the sun, but yesterday's news is over, finished, done with. I have had to send my people out with

75

instructions to wangle something out of somebody, some-how."

"Do you expect any success?"

"It's early days, but I have my hopes." He looked up as one of the later boats was turning to run down the spur into the water. "Those two have been in the wars. One's almost red-raw with sunburn and the others got a plaster at the corner of his mouth."

"I've seen several who are burned. Even their lower lips are not escaping. I saw two applying salve in the clubhouse."

"It's going to sting if they capsize. Salt water will play merry hell with the sore patches."

"Do they often capsize?"

"I believe it's very common if there's a tidy wind. But I don't know whether breezes as gentle as this will upset them very often."

They turned towards the clubhouse as the final few stragglers made their way to the launching points. "There's another with a sore mouth," said Wanda.

"Sunburn?"

"I don't think so. A little abrasion at the corner. Not bad enough for a plaster, anyhow."

"I suppose all parts of their anatomies take a bashing," said Masters. "Heads on booms, knees on thwarts, hands trapped, flying ropes whipping about."

"Obviously a dangerous hobby," said Wanda with a smile. "I must make sure Michael doesn't take it up."

"He could do worse," said Masters. "They seem to me to be fit specimens. Cheerful, too. Exercise and open air must be good for anybody."

Tip had been approached by Liz.

"Is he very important?"

"Who?"

"Your boss."

"Detective Chief Superintendent Masters? He's generally reckoned to be the leader in his field."

"And what's that exactly?"

"The investigation of murders."

"He seems very nice."

"He is."

"I mean he's nicer than you'd think a man with a job like that would be."

"He doesn't commit the murders," said Tip drily.

"I suppose I sound silly to you, talking like that."

"Not at all. Mr Masters is very kind to me and considerate of everybody as far as I can tell, but I must confess I'm a little in awe of him. Not afraid, exactly, but he is so professional that I sometimes wonder if we're in the same job."

"Is he going to find out how Jimmy was killed?"

"He knows how, or should I say, what with. The answer to that is poison. The Chief wants to know who."

"Will he be successful?"

"Yes. If you help him."

"Me?"

"You and everybody else here."

"How can we do that?"

"By opening up. Talking about what goes on other than sailing."

"Nothing, not really."

"There must be. Well over a hundred people don't get together regularly without something going on."

"Sex, you mean?"

"That and jealousy, hatred, snobbishness, ambition, greed—all the human failings. They must all be here. A young man like Jimmy Cleveland isn't poisoned without there's some background to the tragedy."

"Well . . ."

"Well what?"

"Oh, nothing. It doesn't concern Jimmy or Harry Martin. They are two of those who as far as I know were never implicated in any ill-feeling or scandals. But what I really came over to ask was whether you would be at the barbecue tonight?"

"Me?" asked Tip with a smile, "or the Chief?"

Liz blushed. "Of course I meant all of you. I only wanted to know because of the catering."

"Where is the barbecue?"

"Here. On the beach just outside, actually. That's where the fires are going to be. Of course, the bars will be open. But if you are coming, will you let me know?"

"I'll mention it to Mr Masters. Perhaps he will let you know himself."

"Lovely."

"But I should warn you he has a very nice wife."

"I know, more's the pity. I saw her in here when she first arrived. Smashing, she looked."

"I'd better know your name, so that I can tell the Chief who asked about the barbecue."

"Tell him Liz. Liz Ballard. He'll know. He helped me with the frozen food this morning."

"I'm sure he'll remember," said Tip.

Chapter 3

ASHLEY HEAD HAD made the arrangement for Harry Martin
to come to the clubhouse to meet Masters. After he had left
the campsite, Head needed to hurry to be there when Martin
arrived. He made the verandah with several minutes to
spare. From this vantage point he could watch the slope from
the road down which Martin had to come from the car park.
At the same time he could see Masters, with what Head
considered to be an above-average bit of stuff, down at the
launch site. It was going to be easy to arrange the meet.

Masters returned to the clubhouse early enough to
introduce Head to Wanda before Martin came into view. As
soon as Head said that the helmsman was approaching, with
his wife, Wanda said goodbye and went off to join Doris and
Michael on the beach in the next bay. "I'll bring Doris back
with me for lunch, darling. Make sure you order some
sandwiches for us if that's what you have to do."

Head introduced Martin to Masters who immediately
asked Mandy to be present during their talk.

"May I ask why I should be present?"

"Do you mean you *are* asking why, Mrs Martin?" Masters
was being perverse because he hadn't liked the tone of voice
in which the young woman had spoken. He couldn't quite
determine why. Too snooty? Perhaps. Because she obviously
imagined one addressed a policeman as a Victorian debu-
tante is popularly supposed to have addressed her mother's
scullery maid? Perhaps. Because he had never cared for the
habit popular among some young women of wearing a pair
of sunglasses not for the purpose for which they were
designed but as some form of decoration for the top of the
head? Perhaps. But chiefly, he supposed, because he

thought that any decent wife would have jumped at the chance of being by her husband's side to offer comfort, by her presence, during an interview conducted by a senior detective investigating a murder.

Masters' tone also seemed to have its effect. It seemed to cause Mrs Martin to have second thoughts. She was not, after all, dealing with a policeman who didn't speak her language. This one obviously did, as his reply to her request for reasons soon showed.

"I intend to talk to Mr Martin, not as a suspect but as a witness to a murder. Even so, such an experience is, and I speak from some considerable experience in such matters, an emotional and painful one. Furthermore, Mr Martin asked Mr Cleveland to sail with him, so I suspect that he has lost a friend: if not a close one, at least one he was willing to spend long sea-hours with. That could be a cause for sorrow. My questions could be annoying or at least searching. But need I go on? At such a time it is better not to be alone if one's partner can be on hand to lend support or even give a prompting word from time to time."

"An altruistic policeman."

"If you like, Mrs Martin, but having heard what I had to say, you don't have to be party to our talk. I simply thought you might like the opportunity to be present."

The young woman turned to her husband. "What would you like me to do, Harry?"

Mandy Martin was a solidly-built blonde. Not fat, or even plump, but strong and weathered with good features and pale blue eyes. Masters guessed she was in her early thirties and gave him the impression that though she liked men well enough, she considered them to be very much the lesser sex, though unwilling to cosset or pamper them on that account. Masters noted that her question to her husband gave him no help at all either by word or inflection.

"I should like you there," he replied.

"Right."

"Will you want me, Chief?" asked Head.

"Have you something you want to do?"

"Yes."

"Good. In that case, ask Tip to join me. She's in the Wet Bar, I think."

"Tip?" asked Mandy.

"A woman detective sergeant. Her name is Tippen, usually shortened to Tip."

"By her friends?"

"And her colleagues. Now, could I suggest we go up to the Dry Bar, which I understand is open, but which I think is virtually deserted. My spies tell me there are comfortable seats up there."

Masters stood aside to let Martin show his wife the way. Except for the duty steward who was reading a book behind the bar, the room was deserted. Two or three women were on the observation platform outside, but Masters guessed they would be no trouble, because they had had a sun umbrella erected and were occupying deckchairs as though they were there for a long sit.

"This corner?" asked Martin.

"Fine."

Masters faced them over a coffee table. To ease the tension he took out his pipe and charged it with Warlock Flake. Whilst doing so, he glanced surreptitiously at Mandy Martin and realised—as he expected—that her difficult attitude could well be caused by fear. Of what she was afraid, specifically, Masters could not, of course, guess. But he imagined it was just a general sense of unease that any woman whose husband was implicated, no matter how slightly, in murder, would feel. And a police interview, he realised, even for the innocent, could be a terrifying ordeal. There was always the feeling that there could be a miscarriage of justice—that some little point might be seized on and built up into a damning indictment by police officers intent on getting a conviction at all costs.

Tip arrived. She sat on the same side of the table as Masters, in the adjoining chair.

"Now we're all here, we'll have our chat." Masters directed his words at Mandy. "This is to be quite informal," he said.

"No notes will be taken or anything of that sort. And I really hope, Mrs Martin, that you will see from all this informality that I don't believe your husband is guilty of any offence at all. I really believe that it was just his bad luck that Jimmy Cleveland died in his dinghy. However, having said that, I think you ought to appreciate that I have every intention of discovering who did cause Jimmy's death, and to that end I shall question Mr Martin very fully and, if necessary, remorselessly. I feel sure you can understand the reasons for that."

Mandy nodded. "I can see that, but it does not mean that we shall enjoy your interrogation or object any the less strongly if your questions are too searching on purely private matters."

"I shall try to avoid all private matters, certainly those of an intimate nature. Now . . . ," he turned to Martin. "I should like to know your movements from the moment you set off from London to come up here."

"Perhaps," said Martin, "I ought to start on Thursday evening. That was when we collected the boat from the club."

"We?"

"Jimmy and I. We got the boat ready, packed the sails in the hull and so forth, put it on the trailer and towed it to my house."

"Why Thursday?"

"Because we were to drive up here on Friday evening. As you know, we are not allowed to do more than fifty miles an hour towing a trailer, so I was anxious to have everything ready for a quick getaway on Friday. Otherwise it could have been an overnight trip."

"Did young Cleveland travel with you?"

"No. He came up in his own car because he was staying the night with his parents in Nortown and then coming on here early on Saturday."

"So you were to do all that rather tiresome driving on your own?"

"No. Mandy spelled me. She's a very good driver. We came

82

up the A1 because we thought there would be less traffic that way than on the M1, and also because we could stop to change over more easily."

"You stopped several times?"

"Quite often, actually. You see, the hubs of those trailers run hot if you're not careful. We'd packed them with grease on Thursday night, but I wanted to make sure they were still all right from time to time."

"I see. When did you get up here?"

"Just before midnight. I'd warned the hotel we would be very late."

"You made very good time. It's three hundred miles from London to here."

Mandy answered the implied question. "Harry usually leaves his office at four o'clock on Fridays. This time he left earlier. I took him to work in the morning in the car. He took a change of clothing with him. I filled up the car during the day. He worked through his lunch hour and then changed out of his suit and left at three. He took the tube to Edgware where I met him with the car and a packet of sandwiches. I drove while he ate, and we changed over first just north of Baldock. The children slept in the back. The motion of the car always sends them off when they're strapped into their safety seats."

"Thank you. Jimmy just came up in his own car at his own speed, I take it?"

"Yes. He'd a lot further to come—right across London from New Malden."

"Of course. So you clocked in at your hotel at midnight. Then what?"

"Saturday is practice day. We brought the boat down here about nine o'clock and got our berth. Jimmy was waiting for us. We sorted things out and about eleven o'clock we launched and had a trial run out to the course. The buoys were already out so we did a couple of rounds, one triangular and one using just two marks. There wasn't much wind so it took a fair time, but we reckoned we'd got her tuned up by then. We even managed to use the spinnaker.

"After that, well, we pulled her out, hosed her down and sorted things out."

"How long would that take?"

"About an hour, I'd say. Most boats were out that day, but they were coming and going at odd times, so we didn't have to wait for the hose or to get up the ramp like one does after a race when everybody finishes within a comparatively short time. So I should think an hour was about right."

"What did you talk about?"

"How do you mean?"

"Was your conversation confined entirely to matters concerning the boat?"

"Our own and others. There's always a topic, you know. Who's going well, who's got a new suit of sails, all that sort of thing."

"Nothing specific? Did Jimmy, for instance, seem quieter than usual, bad-tempered, depressed, complaining . . .?"

"His state of mind, you mean? He was just as usual. I've never known him bad-tempered or depressed. In fact he was a cheerful chap. Not a hearty, if you know what I mean, but down-to-earth with a wry sense of humour. I suppose you'd say he was a fairly typical northerner."

"So everything in the garden was lovely?"

"I think so." He turned to his wife. "You were there when we got back. He was quite cheerful when we were packing up, wasn't he?"

Mandy agreed this was so. "In fact," she said, "he was quite hilarious about the mayor." She turned to Masters. "You see, at half-past-seven on Saturday night the Mayor of Wearbay was coming here to the clubhouse to welcome the Supras officially. Harry and Jimmy had made sure they got back in good time to pack up the boat and then to go off themselves to get cleaned up for the occasion. We were talking about it and Jimmy told us a story about a local mayor who in a speech on some big occasion had said that the people of his borough had made a public convenience of himself and his wife during their year of office."

Masters smiled. "Not the happiest of remarks, but good for

84

a laugh. So Jimmy had no moans or groans at all."

"None at all," said Martin. "He played with the children and appeared very happy. I know they were."

"There was one thing," said Mandy. She frowned in thought for a moment. "Oh, not a moan . . . what was it now? Oh, yes. I remember. When he was packing up he said that one of your ropes was dicey."

"So he did," said Harry. "The mainsheet. I was surprised, because we'd checked everything on Thursday evening and it was all right then."

"What do you think happened to it?"

"No idea."

"I think I know," said Mandy. "Didn't you use it as extra lashing for the boom for the journey up? I know you said that you were keeping all the ordinary lashing for the mast . . ." She turned to Masters. "The mast travels outside the boat, you know. It's so long it goes right over the top, in a U-shaped stirrup at the front, going almost over the top of the car. At the back it is just lashed down, with a white rag tied on the end. Harry wanted extra lashing, particularly at the front, because of the long journey. So he kept all the bits of spare rope for the mast and used the mainsheet to tie the boom. That travels inside the boat, under the cover, but you have to keep it tied down tightly otherwise it could jazz about and conceivably knock a hole in the hull." She turned again to her husband. "The sheet could have perhaps worn through with a bit of friction."

Harry Martin grimaced. "I suppose so. If it did it was my fault. Anyhow, it's a small enough matter. I ordered another one on Sunday evening from the chandler's van. And that reminds me, he was going to bring it down when he came yesterday afternoon, and I wasn't here to pick it up."

"We can get it today. He's certain to bring it again."

"Of course."

"Any more disasters?"

"No. We went off to the hotel to clean up and then came back for the official welcome. After that I had to attend the helmsmen's briefing, here in the clubhouse, in the Commit-

85

tee Room, while all the others were up here in this bar for the party. Then we rejoined them. Jimmy was staying at a friend's house in the town. Friends of his father's I think he said they were. It saved him a week's hotel bill."

"I hadn't heard that. We'll have to have a word with his host and hostess."

"We got down here by eight on Sunday for the first of the trophy races. Jimmy arrived about the same time as us. We were on the water soon after nine. It was a longish race but we were back soon after three. Then we—that is the Supra crews—gave a cocktail party here in the clubhouse for the Cullermouth people who have laid all this on for us. I know it sounds odd to give a thank you party at the beginning of the meeting, but Sunday was the only evening free to hold it."

"How well did you do in the race?"

"Sunday's? We were ninth, which I didn't think was at all bad as Jimmy and I hadn't sailed together all that often."

"Then came Monday."

Martin frowned. "It was one of those days."

"Why do you say that?"

"You know how it happens sometimes. You expect everything is all right and you arrive not suspecting that it isn't. Jimmy was coming down the slope here when Mandy dropped me at the top. She wanted the car, you see, to go and do some shopping. We walked here together and took the cover off and Jimmy asked me for the shackle key. Then I realised I'd left the tool box at the hotel. I'd taken it back with me because . . . well, tools have a habit of going missing, you know, and I didn't want to lose all my spare bits and pieces. It wasn't a great tragedy, of course, because Jimmy had his car in the park. He gave me the keys and I went off to the hotel to get the toolbox. But when I got back to the car park there was an attendant there who reckoned I should pay again. That made me a bit cross and I spent a bit more valuable time telling him what was what.

"I needn't have worried too much, I suppose, because Jimmy was a pretty capable sort of chap and he'd got most things done by the time I got back."

"Was that the end of the minor irritations before you launched?" queried Masters.

Martin gave a short, mirthless laugh. "It should have been, but I suggested that we test the spinnaker. I don't know whether you know about spinnakers . . . ?"

"I don't, except that they are a type of extra sail."

"That's right. At the bow of the craft. Usually brightly coloured. The spinnaker is kept in a chute—a sort of tube under the foredeck. The material is very fine, thin enough to be folded or rolled to go into the chute from which it is hauled to billow out as it comes. A bit like a stage-magician's trick, I always think."

"You pulled it out?"

"Yes. And then we had difficulty in getting it back. Or I had, rather. There was nothing wrong, just that I was all fingers and thumbs, if you know the expression."

"You were probably trying to hurry because it was nearly launch time."

"That was it, I suppose."

Tip asked: "Why didn't you ask Jimmy Cleveland to do it if you were being a bit ham-fisted at the time?"

"I would have done, but he'd gone off to the clubhouse to collect our lunch."

"Which was?"

"Just one of those huge bread baps they have here. Sandwiched, of course. I was having liver and tomato. Jimmy preferred boiled egg. And a tin of coke apiece. Oh, yes, and he wanted a towel from his kit in the changing room. He liked to wear one round his neck as a sweat rag."

"Nothing else in the eats line?" asked Masters. "A tube of mints or a bar of chocolate, for instance?"

"We didn't take chocolate out with us. In weather like this, in an open boat, it melts and gets quite nasty. Mints? I never knew Jimmy suck sweets, and I certainly didn't. But I can see why you asked. You're wondering whether he had a poisoned sweet. I've thought about it, of course, but I am certain he had nothing to eat after we left the shore. Our lunch was still intact and the coke tins unopened when we got back."

"How close are you physically when sailing the dinghy?"

"Very close. Shoulder to shoulder would be the best general way of describing it, because when we are both trapezing we are literally lying out side by side like two people lying out straight in a narrow double bed."

"Trapezing? That is a new word to me in this connection. Would you mind explaining—not too technically, please?"

"If the wind is on the beam, a helmsman will hold his sail in, that is, as near as possible down the centre line of the craft. If the wind is strong enough, this will cause the boat to heel over. If the wind gets too strong, the sail will have to be let out, otherwise the boat will keel over—capsize. However, if the crew can get their weight outside the hull, on the side opposite from the way it is heeling, one can hold the wind and not capsize. This means the boat can be driven along faster."

"A balancing of forces, in fact?"

"Exactly. Getting weight outside the boat—right outside—is accomplished by using a trapeze, which is merely a body harness fastened high up the mast by a thin but strong wire. This takes the weight of the trunk. The feet are merely held inboard by toestraps. So, literally, the whole weight of either one or both of the crew can be used to counteract the force of the wind that is trying to capsize the boat, while at the same time making use of that same force to drive the boat along. That is trapezing."

"I think I understand that. You lie out literally side by side. So, I presume, the bigger and heavier the crew members are, the greater the use they can make of this manoeuvre?"

"Quite right. In fact, a few years ago, some people started having themselves waistcoats made of several thicknesses of blanket material. Very absorbent. When the need came to trapeze, they just dipped the upper portions of their bodies into the water, and the material soaked up enough to make a significant difference to their weights. As soon as the yachting authorities got to hear of it, they banned it. But you can imagine what an advantage it could be to be relatively light in the boat and much heavier—by about a stone apiece, I seem to remember—outside it."

"Unfair practice?"

"Most people thought so."

"So, to return to Monday morning. What next?"

"It was an ordinary race—for the Smithers Plate. We launched fairly late in the queue. That didn't signify too much, because the fleet was a bit smaller than on Sunday."

"Why was that?"

"Some people came for the weekend, raced on Sunday and then went home. They left their boats, of course, because as far as I know they were all coming back later in the week for the more important races, particularly the King's Cup on Thursday."

"Why is the most important race not right at the end of the week?"

"Just because it *is* the most important race, and the longest. If the weather is unsuitable on the Thursday, it at any rate leaves a chance of it taking place on the Friday. After all, that's mainly what the overseas crews come for."

"I see. So the fleet was slightly smaller on Monday. You got out to the start line on time?"

"With some minutes to spare before the preparatory signal was hoisted. That's the one that means five minutes to go before the starting signal. The warning signal was already up, of course, but that goes up five minutes before the preparatory, so we were all right, but with these fixed line starts, it's a matter of pretty fine judgement to be up close to the line but not across it when the start goes up."

"Jockeying for position?"

"That's right. But you haven't only to watch the start line. You have to stay clear of other craft and make sure you don't get too close up on either side. On one side you could be faulted for pinching another chap's wind while on the other you could be robbing yourself of your own motive power. It's a bit of a musical chairs situation, governed by a stop-watch."

"I can imagine. And you, as helmsman, had the responsibility?"

"Quite right. But Jimmy was a good crew. He could read a helm's mind."

"Because he was a helm in his own boat, usually?"

"That's exactly it. He was probably a better helm than I am."

"Was he? Did you ever let him take over?"

"Quite often. Once or twice in every race he'd take over, and a very good job he'd make of it, too."

"Did he helm on Monday?"

"I handed over for the second round. That is the oblong part of the course, with only two legs round two buoys. I'd helmed the first round."

"Three legs on a triangular course?"

"That's right. He took over for the run after rounding the third mark, and that was quite uneventful. You know what I mean by run?"

"Running before the wind?"

"That's it."

"I don't think I know what it means, Chief."

"I'll tell you in wives' talk," said Mandy, "then you're more likely to understand. When you marry a club member you make it your business to learn the basic terms of sailing or you'll spend your life wondering what the hell he's talking about."

Tip thanked her, and Masters felt pleased that Mrs Martin had by now calmed down sufficiently to add to the conversation in this way.

"You heard Harry talk about a run. Well, running is merely going along with the wind blowing from directly behind the boat, over the stern. When this happens they have the sails fully out, at right angles to the boat. Then there's reaching. That's when the wind is coming over the beam or side of the boat, and then the sail is kept roughly half out. Finally, there's beating. That means sailing directly into the wind, that's when the sail is pulled in hard, or close-hauled, and when they have to tack to and fro in order to sail in a straight line. And talking of tacking, that's the term used when the bow of the boat passes through the direction of the wind, not to be confused with jibing. That's when the boom swings across when the boat is turned out of the wind."

90

"And Mr Cleveland took over for the run between two marks?"

"That's right," agreed Martin, "but that also meant that when we had rounded the downwind mark we then had to come back on a beat—a dead beat, in fact—which is arguably the most difficult part of sailing, because you have to claw yourself along. And it was just as we were starting the beat, having rounded the mark, that Jimmy collapsed."

"Tell me what happened," asked Masters quietly.

"It's not easy to remember," replied Martin. "You see, I didn't know what was wrong. The boat just lost way and started to pay off. I was busy with my own job and it was this sudden move of the boat caused by Jimmy letting go of the helm and the mainsheet. Nothing was under control, you see. My first thought was to grab everything within sight and regain control. But Jimmy had flaked out and his body was in the way. Then, of course, there were the other craft that had rounded the mark just abreast or behind us. We started cutting across them and people were shouting and cursing."

"So what did you do?"

"I eased Jimmy's body into the hull so that he wouldn't fall out and then lowered the mainsail. By this time people were beginning to realise something was wrong, so when I stood up and started to wave and call for help there was a lot of looking round and shouts asking what had happened. Then the American doctor pulled in alongside."

"Dr Jason Humpelby?"

"That's the one. His daughter was crewing for him and she's some sort of medic, too. They drew alongside and he took a quick look and then ordered me to change places with him. Almost immediately he stood up and signalled to one of the rescue launches which had come up and was standing just off from us."

"Please go on."

"I was pretty well-occupied keeping the boat steady while Humpelby moved about. I was keeping the two together, his and mine, by hand. The daughter was in very earnest conversation with her father, and though I didn't understand all the medical talk, I did gather that something pretty diabolical had happened. Then the safety boat surged up and the boats were charging about in the water as they transferred Jimmy on to the bigger craft. I got back into my own boat as soon as that happened. Humpelby demanded that the rescue launch should tow me back to land, and he asked his daughter to sail their own boat in. And that's what happened. I had my sails down, so I just sat in the stern with the tiller and tried to keep a steady line as we came in. I could see Humpelby was working on Jimmy all the way in, but I couldn't see exactly what he was doing as it was all going on below the level of the launch's transom."

"Then what?"

"The beach party hauled me in and helped me to get into my berth on the dinghy park. But I had hardly started to pack up before I was surrounded by policemen and chaps with bottles and apparatus . . ."

"The forensic team."

"Yes. And photographers and so on. I was asked to stand by for a bit, then a police officer told me Jimmy was definitely dead. Poisoned, he said."

"Then what?"

"They asked me to leave the boat and go into the committee room to tell them what had happened. When I got away, the boat had been snugged down and I was told I couldn't use it again. Couldn't touch it, actually, and they had a policeman on duty to see that I didn't. So I just came in here and got a drink, to wait for Mandy to come back with the car."

Masters turned to Mrs Martin. "You came back and found him . . ."

"In a fair old state, I can tell you."

"Naturally."

"So I made him have a stiff drink. Just as well I did, actually, because one of your people—that man Head, it was—came in and started to question Harry. The questions were not . . . well, nice."

"In what way?"

"It wasn't what was actually said or asked. It was the way it was done. Accusingly, I suppose you would call it. As if they thought they had got Harry on the ropes, groggy, and intended to finish him off."

"But not by overtly foul blows?"

"Not foul, but definitely merciless, and that's why I didn't fancy talking to you this morning."

Masters frowned. "I'm sorry that happened. But your husband was alone with young Cleveland . . ."

"Which fact should have immediately suggested that Harry should be the last person to be suspected, not the first. I mean to say . . ."

"Sometimes the obvious answer is the correct one," said Masters gently.

"Oh, what's the use! You're all the same."

"At least they didn't arrest Mr Martin."

"No, but they left him in no doubt he was not out of the wood."

"Directly? Did they say so, I mean?"

"Not exactly. But there was a warning not to leave Cullermouth and to keep himself available for questioning, and a lot more in the same vein."

"I see. I should explain that such injunctions are almost a formula at such times."

"I can't see you using formulas."

"Perhaps not. But I assure you that Detective Inspector Head is a very reasonable man and would not want to antagonize either you or your husband. This time, perhaps, he felt extremely worried, and that can harden the voice. Jimmy Cleveland was the son of his boss, you know, and so, apart from the usual concern of any policeman to resolve a serious case, his feelings for a man whom he holds in the highest regard were probably affecting his attitude. I suspect they still are, but the responsibility was his at the outset where it is now mine, and I imagine that were you to meet him again you would find a noticeable difference."

"That sounds reasonable enough." said Martin, but his wife remained sceptical. "I got the impression we were considered a lesser species because we are southerners."

Masters laughed. "I know exactly what you mean. They treated me a bit like that when I first met them, but I soon learned that it's because they think *we* regard *them* as a lesser species that they put up that particular front. When they learn better, they act just as normally towards us as we do among ourselves and as they do among themselves."

Mandy Martin seemed slightly mollified by this explanation. To further reinforce the good work, Masters said: "Shall we have some coffee, or something stronger, if you'd prefer it?"

"A soft drink, please."

At a nod from the DCS, Tip got to her feet.

"Two lagers and two orange juices? I can get them up here."

"Make it three lagers, sergeant," said Head, coming through the door and overhearing her question.

"Ah, Ashley," said Masters, "come and join us."

Head grinned. "I was about to, Chief." He turned to Mandy. "We've met already this morning, but I don't think I asked you to forgive the rig-out. I'm acting under orders. This is the dress of the day."

Mandy stared at him until he reddened under her gaze, then she laughed. The tension broke. "You've got the right legs for it," she commented. "The left one looks like a tree trunk."

Head was startled. "The left one?" he said, standing up to look at each in turn.

"Oh, and the right one, too. I can see now."

He grinned at her. "You had me worried for a minute, Mrs Martin. Thought I must have caught elephantiasis."

"Instead of which you have caught—what?"

Masters sat back quietly enjoying this *rapprochement*. One of his obsessions was that there should be general good feeling between police and public: that half of police work would be done if mutual trust, understanding and respect prevailed; if even senior officers, frequently divorced from contact with the man-in-the-street, could get along as well with him as the old-fashioned village bobby is reputed to have got along with those on his patch.

"Caught?" queried Head. "Why now, Mrs Martin, I haven't caught so much as a cold."

"But you are a lot happier than you were yesterday at this time."

Head frowned. "Was . . . was I a bit heavy-handed?"

"Just a touch."

Head accepted his lager from the tray Tip had brought over. "Don't answer that, sir," she said to him. "Mrs Martin must know that we all of us have our off-days, particularly under pressure of work. Don't you?" she asked the other woman as she handed her a glass of orange juice.

"Well . . ."

"Of course you do, Mandy," said Harry Martin. "We were scared stiff, yesterday, and Mr Head was faced with what looked like an intractable problem. Hardly conducive to an amicable meeting, was it? The scent of fear and an air of angry bafflement."

"An explosive mixture," agreed Masters. He lifted his glass. "Good health, everybody." After all had responded, he turned to Martin. "I think we can say the business part of our conversation is over. But only for the moment. I have little doubt that we shall need to talk again and so, at the risk of making your wife a little cross, I must ask you to be available at all times. But should you wish to go off for any reason, please say so. We shall not be obstructive, but we'd like to know how to get hold of you, or when."

"We have our two children here," reminded Mandy.

"Where are they at this moment?"

"On the beach with one of the other wives. People are tending to make up parties with just one or two in charge while other mothers have an hour or two off to look at shops and buildings. But we've promised our two they'll be taken to one or two places. I would have been taking them while Harry was sailing, but now they'll expect their father to come with us."

"Of course. As I've said, just let us know you're going. We'll try not to interfere with your trips."

"Thank you."

A few minutes later, the Martins left the bar. As soon as they were away, Head turned to Masters.

"I've turned up some gossip, Chief. By chance, actually."

"What about?"

"Goings on among the men and women here."

"Tell me."

Head recounted how he had met the women in the caravan, and in order to get them talking, had pretended that an older woman attending King's Cup Week had given the police a report about a bit of marital infidelity.

"What was the result?"

"One of those present—Clare Somebody-or-other—blew up. She thought I was referring to an affair of her own with one of the crew members, and she said 'that old cat Vera Bartram has been spreading her poison again, hasn't she?' I didn't try to follow it up, Chief, because I didn't want to antagonize the other women there, and I didn't know whether you would want me to waste time trying to find out who jumps into bed with who."

"I said everything and I mean everything," said Masters. "Get hold of this Vera Bartram and see what she can tell you. Tip, I want you to work on this, too. Get matey with those wives in the kitchen to see if they can help. Not specifically about this Clare person—for whom, incidentally, you'll have to supply a second name—but also about any of them who are enjoying a bit of hanky-panky. I'll explain why. The kitchen people are all members of the Cullermouth Club, so though they might not be too forthcoming with gossip about their own friends up here, they could be less reticent about the southern visitors."

"Is that important, Chief?"

"It could be. Everybody close to Jimmy Cleveland is from the south, so there is a likelihood that the one we're after comes from the south."

"But will these northern wives know . . ."

"You're forgetting they meet up a good many times a year at open meetings. So they know the southerners pretty well, and as onlookers at those weekends they could probably see more of the fun and games than some might think."

"Got it, Chief."

As Tip and Head rose to go, Green appeared. "Ah, there you are, Ashley lad. I'd like a word before you disappear."

Tip said. "I'll get along, Chief."

The three men sat down.

"What's the trouble?" asked Head.

"Local knowledge required, son. I've heard from no less a person than Stan that there was a bit of bad blood among the members here over the furnishing of this club. Apparently one chap is a furnisher in a big way, and another is a furnisher in a much smaller way. When it came to supplying this tidy drop of carpet and the chairs et cetera, the big boy could buy and sell more cheaply than the little boy . . ."

"On account of a bigger turnover, you mean?"

"Right. And that caused a bit of ill-feeling, because the orders to fit out the place were not split, so the big boy got all the profit, all the kudos and, apparently, all the attendant PR that has resulted in scads of sales to other members for their home furnishings."

"And so the little man is sore?"

"It goes further than that," grunted Green. "Word has it that as big boy's bank balance has grown fat, his wife's girth has increased to meet it, whereas little boy's missus has remained pretty slim and attractive."

"I get it. So big boy has now got his eye on little boy's missus, and as he's able to afford some of the luxuries that are missing from her life, little boy's missus has not been averse to seizing her opportunity."

"Correct. So, Ashley lad, get to work. Local firms, both of them. Right up your alley."

Masters nodded. "It's worth looking into, though it blows the lid off my tentative theory that visitors from the south are those more likely to be implicated. See what you can dig up,

Ashley. The Race Office will provide lists of names."

"Right, Chief. I'll get on to it right away."

"Then liaise with Tip over the other business. She should be able to take most of that off your shoulders. But I'll leave it all in your hands."

"Thanks."

After Head had left them, Green asked what the other business referred to might be. Masters brought him up to date.

"Now what?" asked Green eventually.

"More of the same, Bill. We're still dog-paddling around, just getting the feel of things, and for the moment there's nothing more I can suggest we do. For myself, after lunch, I shall have to consult the books to learn a few things about cyanide."

"We've never met it before, have we?"

"No, thank heaven. What little I do know about it gives me the horrors. And when I think of a supply of it probably sculling around loose in Abbot's Haven, with all this food and drink about, I'm just a little scared."

"Me, too." Green glanced across at the picture window facing him. All he could see from his position deep in an armchair was sky—lovely blue sky, lit from somewhere by a golden light, the source hidden but the effect such as to make a man glad to be alive and at ease. Just somewhere, far away and very high up, was a faint wisp of white stratiform, no more than as if a duster had left the faintest of faint smears on an otherwise clean skylight. "In this weather, too! It makes you sick to think of villainy in weather like this. I tell you, George, it's done my heart good to be here today. Oh, I know this building and the car park and the tractors and so on spoil the natural beauty a bit, but the headland and sea are still there, and the kids are running about with just shorts and sun hats on. Marvellous little brown bodies they've got and they're all so unthinkingly happy. Come to think of it, some of the young mums haven't got much more on than their kids and they make up for this concrete box having been dumped in the bay. Abbot's Haven! I'll bet it was quite something when the old God-botherers used to bring their favourite tipple ashore here, before there were roads and motor cars, and only horses and donkeys to ferry the stuff into the Abbey cellars under the cliff."

Masters grinned. "I've no doubt men were just as vile in those days, Bill, and they hadn't got people like us to sort out some of their problems for them, or doctors to heal them and drugs to kill pain. The kids you were talking about, running about all brown and well-nourished, would probably be undernourished, with rickets and earache that couldn't be cured, while a lot of the mums would probably have died giving birth to them. And their men probably killed each other off with daggers or scythes or pitch forks while footpads waylaid travellers for what they had in their purses."

"Just like today, in fact," grinned Green. "Only we call them muggers."

"Quite. Still, it is good weather. Thirsty weather. Would you like a long, cool drink?"

"I thought you'd never ask," replied Green, standing up to take cigarettes and matches from his pockets before fetching a clean ashtray from a nearby table. "Iced lager, George, please."

Chapter 4

"I THOUGHT WE'D find you here," said Berger, coming into the Dry Bar with Sandy Finch.

"Where the beer lurks there lurk I," said Green lazily from the depths of his armchair.

"Even I know that's Shakespeare," said Berger.

"Wrong lad. A parody. *After* the Swan of Avon, if you like."

"What's going on, Chief?" demanded Berger. "Have you wrapped up the case or something? I mean, when the DCI starts throwing poetry quotes at us, it's usually a sign that we're getting somewhere."

"It's the weather," replied Masters. "It has engendered a state of euphoria."

"I see."

"But to answer your other question, no, we haven't wrapped up the case, but we're getting on."

"You could have fooled me," said Green.

"Get yourself and Mr Finch a drink, sergeant," said Masters, handing Berger a fiver.

"And I'll have another, too, lad," said Green. "This sand gets in your throat."

Berger went to the bar.

"Well, Sandy, what have you got for us?" asked Masters as the local DCI sat down.

"Not as much as I'd like to have, Chief, but I've got the complete list of names with addresses and occupations of all but three of them. Oh, and the clubs they sail with."

"Anything else?"

"One or two bits and pieces on some of them, but it's slow work. I've been on the phone all morning—long distance calls, too."

"Do we know which of them are married?"

"Most. One or two divorcees. One or two appear to be quite wealthy, too. But getting facts for so many . . ." He shrugged. ". . . It's like drawing teeth on the conveyor belt system."

"I'm sure it is." Masters was examining the carefully-typed columns Finch had handed to him. "This is very good. Just what I wanted . . . well, almost."

"What's wrong?" demanded Finch.

"Nothing with what you've done so far. It's me. I've thought of something else I'd like."

"What's that?"

"Their journeys abroad in the past year or two."

Green sat up. "Now what's biting you, George? You've got some hairbrained idea sculling round that head of yours. What is it? Or don't you want to tell us in case we get to know something?"

"There's nothing mysterious about it," replied Masters good-humouredly. "I don't know a lot about cyanide, never having met it before."

"The effects or the substance itself?" asked Finch.

"Oh, the substance itself. I think we all know roughly what it does and how quickly it acts. I was thinking more of its availability."

"Like where did our murderer get it from?" asked Green.

"Just so. I don't imagine it is all that easy to get hold of in Britain, but I have an idea at the back of my mind that, years ago, I read that it is much easier to get hold of in quite a lot of foreign countries. That's why I said earlier I would have to consult the library on this particular point, among others."

Finch scratched his close-cropped head. "It's not going to be easy finding out which of this lot has been overseas lately, Chief. It will mean hours on the phone again."

"No, Sandy. I don't want that. You'd be rousing all sorts of unnecessary suspicions by doing that. Do it by asking innocuous questions around here."

"How do you mean, Chief?"

"Start talking to people and bring up the subject of holidays. Ask them if they've ever been to Greece or

Casablanca or wherever. Try the women. They'll tell you. People like talking about how much they enjoyed themselves in Yugoslavia or Cairo. Say you've always wanted to go to Italy or Spain and see what they say. They'll know where all their immediate friends have been. It wouldn't surprise me if you were to get a pretty full list from as few as half-a-dozen informants. But co-opt everybody's help. Berger, Tip, Ashley . . . everybody, including myself and Bill Green. But you collate it into these excellent notes you've got here."

"Understood, Chief."

Masters turned to Berger. "Have you got a list of the berth allocations yet?"

"Yes, Chief. But I thought I'd draw it out. You'll be able to see who was where much more easily that way."

"Good idea. I'd like it before the end of the day on decent paper. If you have to, take the car to a stationer in town to get a big enough sheet on which to make it easily readable."

"Go to a wallpaper shop, lad," counselled Green, "and buy a roll of good, solid, flat-surfaced paper. You can use the back of it for your drawing."

"Ta! Good idea. I'll cut out the shape of a little boat in plastic or cardboard and use it as a template."

"You're learning, lad. Got a fag on you?"

"You mean I have to pay for the idea?"

"All knowledge and experience costs, son. You must have learned that by now."

"Hello," said Tip as Liz, the keeper of the kitchen stores, once more paid a visit to the chest freezer. "More food for the kids?"

"Not this trip. It's meat and stew packs I'm after. We'll have to be getting the casseroles in the oven now."

"Casseroles?"

"For the crews when they get back."

"In weather like this? Casseroles?"

"They wolf it down. I don't know what it is about the briny ocean that whets their appetites for stew so much. I haven't noticed it whetting their appetites for other things quite so much, if you know what I mean. In fact, it dulls them down. After a day's racing all they want to do is eat, drink and sleep. All that lot will be yawning their heads off by half-past-eight tonight."

"Fresh air and exertion, perhaps," suggested Tip.

"Could be. I've accused my old man of making a mistress of his boat and he didn't deny it."

"Here, let me help." Tip took the large, opaque bag of diced beef to allow Liz to forage for similar bags of mixed vegetables for stews.

"There, that should be enough. Sally is making dumplings. They should make it all go a bit further."

"Shall I carry this to the kitchen?"

"If you don't mind, it would be a help. It's getting close to feeding time for the kids, so things are hotting up. Lucy is doing their cooking, but there's more than enough for everybody to do." She led the way out into the passage and round to the kitchen door. "I don't suppose you'd like to help peel the spuds?"

Tip laughed. "I'd get shot if my Chief saw me taking time off for that sort of thing."

"Time off? Pardon me for saying so, but peeling spuds seems to me to be a lot harder work than anything you appear to be doing at the moment."

"Maybe, but my boss wouldn't think so."

"That gorgeous Mr Masters?"

"The same."

"He's pretty dishy."

"He's got a pretty dishy wife, too."

"I know. Isn't it a shame? If he was running around spare, like, I wouldn't mind trying to entertain him myself."

Tip laughed. "No disrespect to you, but I don't think you'd get very far."

"Meaning he hasn't got a roving eye and wandering . . ."

"Exactly that."

"You mean you've tried it on?"

"No. Apart from the fact that the police take a pretty

103

serious view of senior male officers making plays for junior female ranks, he has no time for any woman other than his wife. And I mean that. They make a pretty good advertisement for marriage."

"Still, you must have thought . . ."

"Actually, no. When I first met him I was too much in awe of him to bother about that sort of thing, and by the time I overcame my fears, I'd learned that it would be no use anyway. Shall I put this meat somewhere or do I have to hold on to it for ever?"

"Here, give it me."

"Actually," said Tip, handing over her burden, "I was on an errand to the Chief Super when I stopped to talk to you."

"What was it? Anything exciting?"

"Not really. Just somebody's name."

"Which somebody?"

"Her first name is Clare."

"Clare? Is she tenting or vanning on the camp site?"

"I think she is."

"Then it's Clare Bascombe."

"Mrs or Miss?"

"Mrs. Married to David Bascombe, but very pally with a chap called Dicky Seabright."

"When you say pally?"

"The ultimate."

"I see. It's an open secret, is it?"

"Not really. I know, because my old man, Ted Ballard—I'm Mrs Ballard—caught them at it once down at Chichester. In a bunk house, would you believe! Ted said he was much the most embarrassed of the three and beat so hasty a retreat he blacked his eye on the doorpost. He told me only because I naturally wanted to know about the eye, but I'm sure he's never told anybody else and I certainly haven't."

Tip swung herself up on to the table as Liz took scissors to open the bags. "I'm going to pressurize the meat for a bit before I put it in the oven with the veggies. I think it tenderizes it a bit."

"Good idea. But seeing you've been so helpful over Clare

Bascombe, could you tell me where I could find Vera Bartram?"

"Yes, dear. About two and a half miles beyond the end of the quay."

"Somebody told me she was old."

"Not so. She just looks it. There is a rather elderly woman helming her own boat out there. Mrs Selby. Rather wealthy, I think. At any rate she has a chauffeur/gardener/cum handyman who also crews for her. They never come anywhere in the placings, of course, but they go all over the shop to race, at any rate in the spring and summer. But Vera Bartram's only about five years older than me. Mind, she's got skin like a Gladstone bag and only about as much flesh on her bones as would make a dinner for a Chihuahua suffering from anorexia nervosa. She's a bit of a religious freak, I think. At any rate, she's as hard as little nuts and frowns on any behaviour that's the least bit post-Victorian."

"She sounds a nice character."

"Oh, she is. All for the wheel's kick and the wind's song with deep breathing in between. She frowns on all this . . ." Liz waved her hand, ". . . because she's Vegan or worse."

"A gossip?"

"I'd have said not. I think she has the sort of eagle eye that spots when anybody steps out of line, but she wouldn't speak to other people about it. She'd go straight to whoever she reckoned was the guilty party and tell them to their face."

"I see. Well, thanks. Sorry I can't help with the potatoes, but I've one or two more chores to do."

"Some people have all the luck."

"You're a volunteer here, aren't you?"

"Yes."

"Why do it, then?"

"What? Miss the chance of seeing all these gorgeous men at their hulking best and being in a position to pander to them?"

Tip laughed. "It seems to me you read too many pre-Shakespearian plays at school."

*

Wanda parked the Jaguar close to the entrance to the camping ground. She turned to Doris in the seat beside her. "Just about right for lunch, I expect."

"Ice-cream," said Michael from his safety seat at the back.

"Sandwiches first, I think, young man," said Wanda, unstrapping and lifting him out.

"Sanidges and ice cream," agreed Michael as he was set down.

"Do we need the buggy?" asked Doris.

"I think he can walk on the reins."

They made their way slowly along the length of the car park, across the road and down the slope to the last few feet of churned-up sand before the steps into the club.

"Is it all right for us to go in?" asked Doris. "We're not members."

"We are, so George says. Temporary ones for the whole of the week."

Wanda had been in the Wet Bar earlier, but by now it had been rearranged and transformed. The square, red-topped tables had been pushed together to form two very long ones down the middle of the floor. Places had been set and chairs lined up along their lengths. The chairs were rapidly being filled under the guidance of mothers and helpers.

"It's like a Sunday-school treat," whispered Doris. "Just listen to the noise. It's deafening."

Evidently others thought so, too. One of the helpers stood on a chair and banged a tin tray to win attention and silence.

"Hands up those who like sausages."

A great many small hands were lifted and counting began.

"Hands up those who like beefburgers."

Even more hands went up.

"This is ridiculous," said the helper. "They're all the same ones."

"You asked if they liked them," said a mother. "You should have asked which they would like."

"Okay, we'll start again," shouted the helper. "You can have sausages or beefburgers. Not both. Now, who wants sausages?"

The matter was sorted out more or less satisfactorily, but there was more to come.

"Who likes baked beans?"

Up went the hands again.

"Sarah," screamed one mother, "you know you don't like beans. Put your hand down."

"Thomas," shouted another mum, "you know you like baked beans. Put your hand up, for heaven's sake."

Wanda looked at Doris. "I didn't think old-fashioned school treats were like this. I always understood that the children ate what they were given."

"That's right. Usually tea-cakes cut open with a buttery knife. They were always stingy with the butter, though in those days I must say the tea-cakes had lots more currants in than they do today."

"Is your child going to have lunch with us?" a woman asked Wanda.

"I'm sure he would have liked to, but I've already arranged for us to have it with his father."

"Very wise."

"Thank you all the same."

The smile on the face of the woman was replaced by a look of horror. The reason was becoming increasingly evident. One boy, somewhat older than most present, had started to tap on the table with his knife. One or two others had followed his lead and then, as if under the baton of a conductor, the entire assembly had joined in. With gusto.

"Stop it, you little terrors," shouted the helper who had been talking to Wanda. She darted away, rushing down between the tables, trying to restore order. The mothers broke away from the knots in which they had congregated round the edge of the room and added the weight of their authority. Somewhat vainly. About forty little tots, grinning, laughing, shouting and banging, paid no attention. It was the best game they'd had all day. Bouncing up and down on their chairs, they defied the older generation.

"The only thing that will stop that little lot is food," said Wanda. "Come along, Doris, we'll beat a retreat upstairs."

"Before we're driven out of our minds," agreed Doris. Wanda lifted Michael and led the way.

"Hello, love," said Green to his wife when they reached the Dry Bar, "I thought I heard you coming. Were your teeth chattering?"

"Forty or so perfectly nice children, individually, are committing an affray down there. You should be arresting them, not sitting here drinking beer."

"Lager, love. Have the kids got all the usual? Posters, banners, coshes, petrol bombs, half-bricks?"

"Knives," said his wife.

Green sat up. "Knives, did you say?"

"Yes, knives. It's bedlam down there."

Masters, who had got to his feet to greet Wanda and Michael, asked, "Are they making their demands clear?"

"Painfully audibly."

"What are they?"

"Food for the masses. I think they are insisting on beefburgers *and* sausages for lunch, instead of either/or."

"I see. Will the tumult and the shouting soon die?"

"Only when the plates are put in front of them."

"I think I detect a lessening of the clamour. Due no doubt to Lucy and Liz doing their stuff."

"Lucy and Liz?"

"The kitchen buffs. They gave me a cup of coffee this morning."

"You'll have to watch him, love," warned Green. "He's chatting up all the birds, ostensibly in the line of duty, but you never know with these women whose husbands are all at sea."

"At sea," repeated Michael.

"That's right, feller. Like the old song says: 'My old man's away at sea, and we shall have a night tonight'."

"Bill!" scolded Doris. "The things you teach that child. They're disgusting."

"Not half as disgusting as . . ."

"That's enough. I'd like a sherry please. A large one."

"Seeing we're at a boat club, love, you shall have a schooner."

They ate the huge baps the helpers had been making up into sandwiches. Even cut into four they were enormous. "When I was a lad," said Green, taking a great bite out of a bully beef and salad triangle, "if I ever tried to eat a doorstep like this, my old mother used to say: 'I see you've got a sore hand'."

"You're talking with your mouth full," said Doris.

"Am I? That's funny, there's nothing there now."

"There was, and you know it."

"You slobbered a bib-full, babe," replied Green with a nasal twang. "Do you remember hearing that in the old American films, love?"

"I don't remember such things."

Finch asked, "Is this how you lot usually carry on at lunchtime?"

"Not really."

"It's just William trying to cheer us up because we're missing our holiday," said Wanda. "He's a great cheerer-upper."

"I can imagine. Well, ladies, if you'll excuse me. And you, Chief. I've got to go and see some people about their holidays."

"I'll be away, too, Chief," said Berger.

"Tip hasn't fed yet. If you see her tell her the food is here. Oh, and catch up Mr Finch. Tell him I'd like him to rejoin us in about a quarter of an hour."

"Right, Chief."

As Berger left, Ashley Head came in. "Any grub left?"

"Help yourself. Leave some for Tip. She's the only one still to come."

"I don't suppose," said Wanda, "that we can ask you how you're getting on?"

"You can ask," replied Green. "I've no doubt George has got it all sussed out, but for the rest of us the answer is nil, zero, nothing. Put it how you like."

"As bad as that, William?"

"As bad as that, love."

"You're a rotten sailor, aren't you, Bill?" asked Masters, cutting in.

"I get sea-sick in the bath, so if you're about to suggest that I should venture out into the middle of the North Sea in a sailing dinghy, you can forget it."

"As you like." Masters turned to Head. "I want to go out to the fleet. Can I get a motor boat to take me?"

"Meaning can I lay one on for you, Chief?"

"Yes, please. With crew, of course."

"Can do. We have a constable . . . look, leave it with me, Chief. When do you want to go?"

"As soon as possible, please. It is now one o'clock and the race will be over by . . ."

"Two, Chief. Maximum four hours and they started at ten. Will tomorrow morning do. It'll give me a better chance to arrange things."

"Right. Tomorrow at nine-thirty? Once they're all away from the launch area."

"Consider it fixed. How many to go?"

"Just the man to crew the boat and you, if you'd care to come. I don't know how long we'll be out."

"I'll be there, Chief."

"Thank you."

Wanda asked, "Do you hope to find something out there, George?"

"Not find, love," said Green. "See."

Masters smiled at his wife. "I've had a thought, darling. I want to test it." He turned to Green, "And before you ask, Bill, we'll discuss it in a few minutes' time, when Sandy gets here. You, too, Ashley. If you'll join Bill and me for a stroll to the end of the quay as soon as you've finished eating."

"Give me five, Chief. I'm going to get a cup of coffee."

After Head had left them, Wanda said, "That sounds as if we should go . . ."

"No, please. Stay here so that Michael can have a rest on one of the sofas, and while you're at it, take care of Tip's food for her. And talk to Tip about any gossip she may have picked up. I'd like your interpretation of it as well as hers. Bill and I will be back in an hour's time and then we'll discuss going home and such like."

110

"All right, darling, but I'm quite happy here. It's quiet now and comfortable and the view from those windows is lovely."

"You'll see the leading boats start coming into the Haven about half-past-two, I expect. Unless the start was delayed, of course, but I can't see any reason why it should be on a day like this."

The quay, a solid concrete and stone construction, ran out for about four hundred yards. The northern side was protected by a solid wall over seven feet high, as a protection for the Haven, and thus the river mouth, from the worst of the winter gales. Along its length ran a set of railway tracks, carrying a large, modern crane, high on four legs so that a laden vehicle could drive underneath its structure. Painted in the yellow so common to so much modern equipment, it was stationary halfway along the quay, its cab empty, with its jib and arms in the 'at ease' position.

"That's a modern piece of machinery," grunted Green. "Is it ever used?"

"The occasional Baltic boat berths alongside here," replied Finch. "It saves the long haul up the river and docking fees, I suppose."

"It's deep enough alongside?"

"When the tide's in, certainly. You can see the bollards. I think it is mainly perishable food that comes in here. Fish, probably, and dairy produce."

"Small craft?"

"That's right. Probably some of our own little coasters carrying holds full of sand and gravel. The sort of thing, that has to be scooped out and loaded on to lorries."

It was obvious that the quay was not only regarded as a weather break and an industrial site. The local council had put benches at intervals for the use of anybody wishing to stroll out to sea. Quite a few of these were fully occupied, particularly by elderly people warming their bones in the heat of the sun. At the end of its run, the quay widened out slightly into a bulbous turning circle. Here the wall lessened to a mere four feet in order, as Finch explained, to allow sea

111

anglers to cast over it. Two boys had their rods and cans of worms and were busy on what appeared to be a fishless exercise.

"Seats here, Chief," said Head. "Will these do? Those lads are far enough away not to overhear us."

"Just the ticket."

"Now," said Green, offering a crumpled packet of Kensitas to Finch, "What's it all about, George?"

"First, let me tell you how I think we now have to proceed. The usual prerequisites apply—means, motive and opportunity. And method, of course."

"Agreed. And the means was cyanide," said Finch.

"Not quite," said Masters. "Cyanide was the instrument—only part of the means. We have to include under the heading of means the method of administering the poison to Jimmy Cleveland."

"I get it. Cyanide was only the weapon."

"That's it lad. The blunt instrument, where the full means would include the wielding of it."

"Let's talk about that a bit more," said Masters, leaning forward on the seat, elbows on knees. "We know that cyanide is a hell of a fast worker. It can kill within a minute. That is one of the properties of the means. But it doesn't quite stop there, because it goes on to overlap into opportunity and method."

"We know," said Finch, "that because it works so fast, it could only have been administered out there on the water, a matter of seconds before young Jimmy collapsed."

"True, but for administered you must substitute ingested. Jimmy only ingested it moments before he died. But administered?"

"The means of putting it where it was certain Jimmy would ingest it," grunted Green.

"Quite right. And the obvious way of doing that would be to put the cyanide in something he was going to eat or drink after he got out on the water."

"That's it," admitted Green, "but we're assured by all and sundry that his sandwiches were untouched—and, in any case, it wasn't grub time—that his can of coke was unopened

112

and that he didn't take any crisps or sweets out with him."

"Exactly. And for reasons which I needn't repeat, we don't think Harry Martin was responsible for giving him anything to eat or drink."

Neither of the two locals commented. After a short silence, Masters went on. "The speed of action of cyanide means that it was ingested out on the race course. As Jimmy Cleveland ate or drank nothing out there, it means that something else happened during the course of the sailing. We don't know enough about the sport to know what that could possibly have been, and the only fact concerning it is what I learned from Martin this morning, and that was that Jimmy had taken over the helm for one of the more tricky legs of the race before he collapsed."

"Ah!" said Green. "That's why you want to go out there tomorrow morning."

"Right. It may be a complete waste of time, but I want to station myself near that particular buoy with a pair of binoculars so that I can see exactly what takes place. Every movement of every person, I mean. It's no good to us to have some sailing buff explain what happens. You know what I mean. 'Well . . . er . . . they round the marker to loo'ard, close-hauled, with the wind on the beam and the helm a'lee, you know. Then they go into a reach and jibe before getting out on the trapeze, keeping their eye on the something or other at the masthead to see how the wind is behaving. All very easy, you know. Nothing to understand, really, you know.' And that's the sort of thing we would get. No good at all to us."

"I see what you mean, Chief," said Head. "I'll see we have two pairs of x10 binoculars with us tomorrow."

"Thank you, Ashley. Now does any one of you disagree with me that Jimmy Cleveland did lots of things simultaneously out there? Took over the helm, changed seats with Martin, rounded a buoy, managed his sails, ingested cyanide and died."

"Even putting it all like that," agreed Green, "clears the thing in my mind. I can picture it."

113

"Me, too," said Finch. "Now we've got to have a little thumbnail sketch like that to show how the stuff was administered."

"True," said Masters. "So let us begin afresh on that problem. The cyanide was put on board the dinghy before it left the shore."

"Before it was launched, Chief?"

"Not necessarily, Ashley, though I suspect so. But all we can be sure of is that it was inboard before the boats separated to go their own ways. From what I saw this morning, once they're in the water they tend to congregate very closely for so long a time that the Beach Master has to chivvy them away. For any one so minded, there would be a good opportunity at that time to drop something . . ."

"Over the gunwhale or transom," supplied Green. "You see, I'm learning the lingo."

Masters grinned. "However, to get back to drawing things together concerning the placing of the cyanide. In the boat park the craft are worked on by day and left securely covered over by night. I am discounting any action by night, because I would assume any raid by local villains would be for the purposes of vandalism or theft—neither of which has occurred to our knowledge—and not for committing what appears to be an extremely sophisticated killing."

"Agree with that," said Finch. "Yobos haven't usually enough nous to disguise their actions."

"So it's a daytime job?" asked Green.

"I'm banking on our man being somebody who is connected with this meeting. Heaven knows that gives us a wide enough field."

Green grunted his agreement with this.

Masters continued. "Just as I propose to go out to the fleet tomorrow, so I have asked Berger to make me a plan of the boat park, with names of helms and crews. It may be unnecessary, but propinquity there could be important. I mean the park is the best part of two hundred yards long, and although the crews are pretty matey, when they are there they tend to work pretty hard on their own craft, probably gassing to the people alongside them, but not parading from one end to the other to swap yarns. My guess is that they give themselves enough time to rig their craft in the mornings, and after they've snugged them down after a race I would judge they would want to be away to attend to other things as soon as possible. So, propinquity in the park could be a factor or, alternatively, we might hear of somebody wandering along the line for no apparent reason. But as I say, though Berger's exercise could be very inconclusive on its own, it could help substantiate other things."

"Such as, Chief?" asked Finch.

"The job you're doing for one, Sandy. I haven't yet looked up the reference books on cyanide, but as I told you, I think it is easier to obtain it overseas than in this country. So, if you can tell me somebody has recently been abroad to one of the countries where cyanide is readily available, and Berger's plans shows me he is placed four boats away from Martin's *Spearhead*, we shall look at him pretty closely. Or alternatively, if your list tells me one of the sailors is a professional pest controller, regularly using cyanide for the taking of wasps' nests, and he's berthed close to Martin, we shall go to town on him."

"If we strike oil by any of this," said Green, "we shall narrow things down considerably."

"That's what I'm hoping for. So, Sandy, that, in part at least, explains your activities and those of Berger. It still gets us no closer to how the poison was administered or how Jimmy Cleveland came to, or was induced to, ingest it. But it will help to know who."

"I'll say it will, Chief."

"Which just about covers the end of the means and methods sections as well as the opportunity bit. So, finally, we have to think of motive. We're all of us experienced enough to know all the emotions that provide so called motives for murder—greed, jealousy, hatred and so on, with financial or sexual connotations. I should add to that a number of mental states that are so abnormal as to drive some people to apparently motiveless crimes, but I have a feeling we can ignore these last in this instance."

"Agreed," said Green. "To me it sticks out that this is some infidelity business. Most of these people are just within the right age brackets to get up to a bit of hanky-panky, and they're all thrown together, away from home, with husbands too interested in their boats to worry what their neglected wives could be getting up to on shore. And the wives being neglected and free to roam . . ."

"That's what I think, Bill, and so that is why I've got you, Tip, and Ashley specifically, and everybody else when the opportunity arises, listening to gossip and trying to pick up titbits of information that could give us a lead to ill-feeling within the group."

"On the face of it," said Green, "they're as happy a bunch as you'd hope to meet, but underneath it's seething."

"As normal," admitted Masters. "You yourself have stumbled on a bit of business jiggery-pokery combined with resulting sexual complications. Ashley has turned something up and Tip is trying to confirm it. And so on."

"I get it, Chief," said Finch. "We get out these lists, and if names appear on all of them, we can put them in the frame."

"Something of the sort, Sandy, but there's one very big consideration we must none of us forget."

"I know," grunted Green. "We've got to be prepared to discover that Jimmy Cleveland was not the intended victim at all, but somebody else who hasn't yet come to mind."

Masters nodded. "That's it, Bill."

"Damn and blast," said Finch. "I'd forgotten that. And if that's how it does turn out, I can't begin to think what Matt and Philippa Cleveland are going to feel about it for the rest of their lives."

There was a moment or two of silence, and then Masters said: "Mr Pedder will probably call up today to see what progress we are making. I shall speak to him if I'm there, but if I'm not, and you can take the call, Sandy, don't tell him everything we've discussed here. He'll be impatient for news and results, but we must not give him—and, consequently,

Matt—any false hopes. Just say we've begun in a way we think is quite satisfactory, but that it is going to take a lot of work to bring things together."

"Which it is," growled Green. "We shall need our bit of luck if we're going to wrap this one up by Friday."

Finch grimaced. "God knows what we'll do if we overrun. Once this lot breaks up it'll be nigh on impossible to conduct an investigation."

"In which case," said Masters, standing up, "it is time we got on with our various jobs. I suggest we all meet at five o'clock in Ashley's office at the police station. We'll have a brain storm session at that time."

"Right," said Finch. "We'll lay that on and mention it to the sergeants if we come across them."

"Thank you."

They started to make their way back along the quay to the clubhouse.

Tip ate her food slowly. Doris Green and Wanda Masters were drinking coffee, watching over a sleeping Michael.

"Liz told you that she and her husband, Ted, had never mentioned the affair between Clare Bascombe and Mr Seabright," said Wanda. "Yet Vera Bartram knows about it. Can you believe that it is not common knowledge?"

"No," replied Tip, "because all the other women in the caravan with Mr Head this morning heard Clare jump to the conclusion that Vera Bartram had been gossiping about her, and according to Mr Head, they showed no surprise about it."

"So it was no revelation to them?"

"I would think not."

"Then," said Doris, "if so many know, everybody knows, and I reckon this Clare Bascombe and her husband will both know everybody knows. So, if you want my opinion, Mr Bascombe wouldn't do anything secret about it, he'd go straight for a divorce. And if I were you, Tip, I'd enquire whether the first steps have been taken in that direction."

"Because if he was likely to get a divorce from Clare pretty soon, he wouldn't want to kill somebody on her account, do you mean?"

"That's exactly what I mean."

"But both Clare and her husband are up here together for this meeting."

"Of course they are. Clare has probably insisted on coming because the Seabright man is here. But it doesn't necessarily mean Bascombe and Clare are together, as you put it."

"You think I should check whether they are?"

"Go into the Race Office and see whether David Bascombe is listed as having either a tent or a caravan on the camp site," suggested Wanda.

Tip nodded. "It does seem as though this particular affair is a little too easy as a motive for murder."

"I think so. You'll have to fish in deeper waters, Sergeant," said Doris. "Find something everybody isn't talking about. That's more likely to be the cause of the trouble."

Tip considered this for a moment. "But if nobody is talking . . ."

"Observation," said Wanda.

"But that's only possible when the men are ashore."

"I'm afraid so. But that's how it will have to be done, in my opinion."

Tip grimaced. "That's a pretty tall order."

"I expect it is. But I see from the programme that there are social functions every evening. That is when things might be observed, so that is when you will have to be on the lookout."

"There's a barbecue here, on the beach, tonight."

"That sounds like an ideal opportunity for you. For you, and as many other observers as you can muster."

Masters found the Yard car was not in the car park, which suggested to him that Berger had gone into Wearbay to buy the paper for his layout of the dinghy park. Expecting the DS back at any time, Masters decided to wait for him. The asphalt of the park reflected the heat of the sun too unpleasantly for Masters' taste, so he strolled down towards the turn-off to the moat and camp site where the trees offered some shade and the grass a comfortable enough seat for a short wait. His sole intention was to find shade so he sought, until he found, a tree that offered deep shadow. The sun was now just west of south, and so when he sat with his back to the trunk, he was facing almost north-east. Just to the left of his field of vision, over the far bank of the moat, he could see the roofs of buildings on the edge of the town. To the right, he found himself looking along the length of the moat and, thus, straight down the grassy track that had been left between the caravans on one side and the tents on the other. There was no movement anywhere. The sleep of the afternoon, the sky immaculate, all steady and still.

To prevent himself nodding off, Masters started to pack a pipe with Warlock Flake. He guessed he would hear the Rover return to its space in the park. As he lit up, he forced his brain, more as an exercise in keeping awake than anything more, to memorize the vans and tents. He carefully noted shapes, colours and sizes and then, closing his eyes, recited them back to himself in order to keep his mind alert. As he reopened his eyes, to check on his own mental test, he saw movement near one of the vans. A man coming from one of them. A man who turned on the step of the vehicle to receive a kiss from a woman who had to bend down to reach him. Masters noted it all very carefully. The man, the woman and the van. Illicit? Masters imagined so, because instead of coming towards where he was sitting, and thus the entrance to the site, the man took to the bank of the moat behind the van and was immediately lost to sight in the bushes there. The woman stood on the top step of the van long enough to glance both ways along the row as if to make sure the surreptitious exit has not been observed. Then the woman withdrew into the van.

Masters, taking what care he could not to appear in the open, moved quietly back to the car park where he waited the few minutes for Berger to arrive.

"You want me, Chief?"

"The keys, actually. I'd like the books from the boot."

The travelling library was a byword. In it, Masters had

119

books on toxicology, pathology, medical jurisprudence, poisons and toxic effects, Martindale's *Extra Pharmacopeia*, Black's *Medical Dictionary* and several other reference volumes, including a gazeteer and a guide to the law. Other investigators had smiled at the idea of a travelling library, but had soon begun to follow suit. Books on weapons were a great favourite, with smaller pamphlets on tyre imprints and the like becoming very popular.

"Where do you want them, Chief?"

"Here, on the back seat, please. Thank you. Leave me the keys, and please discover for me, discreetly, who owns the Sprite caravan, fawn and white, third down in the row, counting from this end. When I say discreetly, I mean nobody is to see you going about the business and nobody is to know of your interest. Except me, that is."

"Right, Chief."

As soon as Berger had gone, Masters turned to the books and started jotting down notes on what he read there.

Somewhat to his surprise the poisons book did not mention cyanide. He guessed that the author, who was concerned with treatment, had decided that in the case of cyanide the chances of treating a case either successfully or in time were nil.

The pathology book was not of much more use, as this featured mainly the autopsy findings after cyanide poisoning. It was a little more informative about the sources of cyanide. But, obviously for the sake of safety, the details were not great. Solid sodium and potassium cyanides are used in industry and are readily available for use in certain hobbies such as photography. Hydrogen cyanide gas is used for fumigation. Prussic acid, which is liquid hydrogen cyanide, is used in industry, by veterinary surgeons and as an ingredient in some medicines.

The medical jurisprudence book was a little more informative. Hydrocyanic acid in laboratories; oil of bitter almonds containing from 5 to 14 per cent of hydrocyanic acid before it is separated off to allow the refined essence to be sold as a flavouring agent; vegetable seeds—bitter almond kernels of cherry, plum, peach, apple pips, cherry-laurel leaves and parts of other plants, mostly belonging to the *Rosaceae*, contain amygdalin, a glucoside which on fermentation yields hydrocyanic acid.

The toxicology book had eleven different page references in the index. Masters chose the general discussion. Average fatal dose about 0.25 grams. A quarter of this amount has caused death. Laboratories, agricultural fumigation and ship fumigation use cyanide, some fertilisers contain calcium cyanide, cyanide solution is used in case-hardening of metals and in electroplating and in the extraction of precious metals.

The *Pharmacopoeia*—Caution: The vapour, when inhaled, is intensely poisonous. After large doses of hydrocyanic acid, unconsciousness occurs within a few seconds and death within five minutes. And there they all were, the foreign countries in whose pharmacopoeias the various cyanide products appeared. Chile, Jugoslavia, Portugal, Spain, Argentina, Australia, Romania, Belgium, France, Switzerland. Would the products be more readily available in the countries where they *were* listed, or where they were *not* listed? Certainly they must be available worldwide. Would those countries that listed them restrict their availability to a greater degree than those that apparently ignored them? Masters could not decide. Events would need to decide for him. He read on. Potassium cyanide soluble in water; potassium ferricyanide, *very* soluble in water; potassium sodium cyanide, soluble in water; sodium cyanide, *very* soluble in water. Many repeats of the first caution: This substance is intensely poisonous. Uses: sodium cyanide, used industrially for extracting gold and silver from ores, for case-hardening metal and in electroplating and photographic processes; potassium cyanide used for similar purposes; ferricyanide, photography, potassium sodium cyanide used by entomologists for killing insects; note of interest, the use of cyanide gassing-powders for the destruction of wasps in houses is illegal. But only in houses? What about in agriculture?

121

Masters closed the book. The reading had tired him because, though he had opened the car windows, the interior was hot and sticky. He would have liked to bathe, to wash away the runlets of sweat he could feel coursing down his back and chest. But he hadn't come equipped for sea bathing. Then he remembered the showers in the clubhouse. If Wanda was still there she would certainly have a towel among all the kit she carried about for Michael, especially on a visit to the seaside. If Wanda had gone, well then he would ask Liz or Lucy in the kitchen for the loan of a towel. He guessed they wouldn't refuse him.

Ashley Head had a great many contacts in Cullermouth and Wearbay. It was to them that he turned for information concerning the rival owners of the furnishing shops that had supplied the new clubhouse. Hunt, he learned, was the man in a big way of business, Claybourn the smaller of the two. He learned that Carol Hunt, the large, flashy wife of Maurice Hunt, apparently didn't give a toss about her husband's social and extra-marital activities just so long as he continued to provide her with the wherewithal to indulge her own expensive tastes in food, clothing, jewellery, cars and travel—usually to London for shopping sprees. Alec Claybourn, on the other hand, according to Head's information, was a more introverted man, very unlike Hunt. Nancy Claybourn, he was told, was a pretty little thing who, as far as anybody knew, stuck by her husband and worked in his shop. It was only after a number of calls that he got any hint of a liaison between her and Hunt. "Hunt's a womanizer," said this last informant. "He's run after any number of women. He's expansive, loud, a drinker, and he'll splash money about on any bit of skirt that takes his fancy." Yes, he'd been running after Nancy Claybourn. He'd been seen in her company. Presumably when Alec Claybourn had been out sailing or spending time at the club. Hunt was the sort who'd forego a day's sailing on Sunday if Claybourn was on the water. He'd stay away to keep Nancy company. Did Claybourn know? As to that, it was anybody's guess, but there was definitely a feeling of animosity between the two men over business matters, at least on Claybourn's part. Hunt was the sort that—on the surface at any rate—would tend to laugh off a defeat in business, such as losing a tender for recarpeting an office block. But he was a keen and shrewd business man who would undercut any competitor if he thought it would pay him to do so. Claybourn, however, was bitter in defeat. Probably because he couldn't afford to be as flexible as Hunt. Until his business grew bigger he couldn't accept the win-some-lose-some philosophy of Hunt. He had to win them all in order to build up into a company of good financial standing. Nancy Claybourn had worked with her husband, but there were rumours that the constant hard work for, as yet, little reward, allied to her husband's soured attitude, was beginning to pall.

Head assimilated all this from various sources, but one fact seemed to him to negate any likelihood of the information being of the slightest use in the investigation and that was that neither Hunt nor Claybourn was a Supra sailor. They both belonged to different classes within the club. Hunt sailed an Enterprise and Claybourn a Mirror dinghy. It was difficult to see how two men, in no way connected with this big Supranational meeting, could be involved in the business surrounding Jimmy Cleveland's murder.

After leaving Masters to do his reading, Berger went to the Race Office. It was deserted except for a girl typist who was sitting at her desk, cutting out and pasting up newspaper clips.

"You keep track of what everybody has to say about things, do you?"

"We keep a diary of the meeting, and it's very interesting to read the different headlines concerning the same day's racing. So-and-so dominates; Somebody-or-other and Somebody-else clear; this one wins; Cup for him and him. Really, you wouldn't think they were talking about the same event."

Berger looked round. There was a spare table with six

correspondence trays on it. They were labelled: Principal Race Officer, Assistant Race Officer, Rescue Officer, Communications, Beach Master and Protest Convenor.

"Would you mind," asked Berger, "if I were to pile these up a bit to make room for a drawing I want to make?"

The girl shrugged. "Everything's up-to-date and done until today's race finishes, so you can help yourself."

"Thank you." Berger stacked the almost empty trays and unrolled a length of his white paper. After finding objects with which to hold it down, he produced his stylized cut-out of a dinghy and proceeded to concoct his dinghy park layout with names, helm at the top, crew at the bottom of each little diagram. The girl finished her pasting-up and came across to watch.

"What do you want that for?"

Berger played his part. "I don't, but my boss does. All bosses get these funny ideas."

"Yeah, I know. Mine does."

"After this I've got to get a list of who's got caravans and tents on the camp site."

"That's easy," said the girl. "I can give you one of those. There's not all that many in there. Five or six vans and about as many tents."

Berger smiled inwardly with satisfaction. "I'll copy them out when I've finished this."

"I'll type a list for you."

"Would you? That'll save a bit of time and labour."

"Anything to help."

"Ta."

The girl put a sheet of paper in her machine. "Are you coming to the barbecue tonight?"

"Dunno. I'd like to, but I never know what my boss is going to want me to do. You never get a minute to yourself in the police, you know."

"Yes, I know. It's awful isn't it? Especially for a married man. Are you married?"

"Never found anybody who'd have me," said Berger, working away at his plan which by now was beginning to fill up. He pretended to consider his next remark. "It's difficult for us, you know. The only women we really get to meet are either criminals or policewomen. And I mean to say, who'd want to marry a policewoman?"

"They get big feet, you mean?"

"Not that so much, but you might wake up one day to find your misses had been promoted above you and the rest of your life you'd be kissing a Police Inspector."

The girl tore the sheet of paper from the typewriter. "When you put it like that it does sound awful, doesn't it? But if you come to the barbecue tonight it would be nice."

"Who for? Me?"

"The two of us, like."

"Won't your . . . er . . . boyfriend be with you?"

"Haven't got one. Well, not a proper one."

"So you'll be alone?"

"Yeah."

"In that case, leave it with me, love. I'll tell my boss I want to do a bit of out-of-hours investigating round here."

"Cheeky!"

"Nothing meant by that, love. I'm a copper, remember. I have to see there's no goings on . . ."

"Pity."

". . . of a nature liable to cause a breach of the peace, I mean."

"I'll look out for you then, shall I?"

"Do that, love. By the way, are you a member of the club?"

"Oh, no. My boss is the Principal Race Officer for the meeting. He asked me to come and look after this office for the week. So I'm sort of honorary and can go to all the do's. He's paying for me."

"I see. I'm sort of an honorary member, too, but I expect I'll have to pay for my own ticket."

"No need. I'll get you a complimentary." She handed him the camp site list. "I'll have it in my bag when you come."

"Thanks. And thanks for the list, too. I've nearly finished this little lot. Just a few more names to put in."

*

Wanda was still in the Dry Bar, talking to Doris and holding Michael up on the low sill of one of the picture windows to see the first boats to cross the finishing line heading into the Haven.

"One or two are already back," said Doris. "They retired from the race for some reason."

"Faulty equipment probably," said Masters. "Something broke under the strain."

He spent a moment or two explaining that he was proposing to take a shower and asking for the towel from Wanda's beach bag. "It'll be a bit sandy, darling. We dried Michael's feet on it."

"No matter. I'll be back in a few minutes."

There was little privacy in the showers, although each one had a cubicle. Masters chose the far one and selected a setting that provided a lukewarm but powerful spray. He stood beneath it, not moving, except to turn to allow the water to sluice both sides of his body. Shortly after he had started, another two men entered the room.

"Two empty," said one voice. "We're lucky, Alan."

Alan replied. "That's the only thing to be said for retiring. You get a shower in peace." Alan sounded rather disgruntled.

"Cheer up." The water started to flow in the cubicle next to Masters, and the voice was raised slightly to overcome the noise. "It's the luck of the draw."

"We were running third," grumbled Alan. "If that trapeze wire hadn't gone . . ."

"But it did. And we weren't catching up. In fact, we were being overhauled by a bunch of other craft. We'd have been crucified on that last leg."

"Rubbish." Another jet started. "Listen, Tim, I think there has been some nobbling going on here."

"How do you mean?"

"Well, first there was young Jimmy Cleveland. And there was Barnaby's spinnaker. A new one! And as soon as he tried to put it up there was a slit in it over two feet long. Then there was our trapeze wire today."

"Come off it, Alan. Nobbling would be somebody trying to stop others winning. Harry Martin wouldn't have led here, this week. Everybody knows that. Sixth or seventh, maybe, but no chance of an overall win. Barnaby used to be the champion, I know, and he can afford a new boat every year, but he's getting on now. He sails for the hell of it. He knows he won't be higher than third or fourth in any race. And as for us . . ."

"What about us?"

"I know you had high hopes, Alan, but were they realistic? I mean, things would have to go wrong for several others to let us in. The Canucks are outsailing everybody. They were a mile in front of us today. As they have been twice before."

"I still think we could have been up there if we hadn't had to retire today."

"Have it your way. We shall need a new trapeze wire, oh, and a cleat before the King's Cup race on Thursday."

"I'll see the chandler. He'll have spares on his van. If not, we'll go into Newcastle and collect them from his store. We can get them fitted tonight."

"Tonight? What about the barbecue? What about that bird you're supposed to be meeting there?"

"What bird?"

"Come off it, Alan. You and Connie Akers. You've been . . ."

"Leave Connie out of this." The tone was venomous.

"Sorry, sport. I didn't know it meant so much to you."

"Just forget it, will you, Tim. And hurry up and get out of that shower. We've got work to do."

Masters stepped out of his cubicle and had nearly towelled down before Alan and Tim emerged. But by that time there were two or three others hanging around, draped in towels, waiting to get under the sprays. He felt gratified by this. He was lost in the crowd. But though Alan and Tim had not noticed him, he had taken stock of them.

After the talk at the end of the quay, Green began to wonder whether Masters was handling this case as it should be handled. Not that Green, after years of working with Masters, was a great believer in the setting up of Incident Centres with clerks, phones, files, blackboards and hordes of duty tea-cups scattered about, but this time . . . well there were a great many people who could or might be involved in the business of Jimmy Cleveland's death, and Green felt that every one should be questioned closely. There would be a lot of dross, of course, but a systematic investigation could probably yield more results than Masters' rather more hit-and-miss methods. Not that Masters was wrong. He rarely was on a job like this, and he had tailored his investigation method to the time at his disposal, but would that work? The way Masters had explained it to him and the two locals, it seemed a result would be a likely outcome, but there wasn't a lot of fact to work on. Masters hadn't disguised that, but such a method as the one proposed, without adequate facts . . .

"Bill! Bill, you're daydreaming."

"Oh, hello, love."

"I saw you through the window. You looked lost."

"Did I? Just thinking, Dolly."

"Now I know you're worried. You never call me Dolly unless you are."

Green grinned. "You should be on this job, not me."

"What do you mean?"

"I'm not sure of things. I think we're all at sixes and sevens."

"Does George think so?"

"Deep down, I think he does. He's putting on a good face, of course, but he's very conscious of how little time he's got and he's so keen to do a proper job for Matt Cleveland and Alf Pedder that he's trying to cut corners."

"That's not like George. He seemed very relaxed when I saw him. Not at all worried, in fact."

Green grimaced but made no comment.

"Isn't there something you can do to help him?"

"Apart from keeping my eyes and ears open, nothing."

"If that's what George has asked you to do, you do it. I'm going back to Wanda and Michael now. If the boy has finished his nap, we're going into town to do some shopping for supper, then we're going back to the cottage."

"Okay, love. I don't know when we'll get there . . ."

"Don't worry, we'll keep supper until you come."

Green stood at the water's edge, trying to think of some way of actively pushing the case along. Masters, after his shower, found him there.

"You're looking pretty gloomy, Bill."

Green turned to Masters. "I've a feeling we're stuck, George."

"Sorry about that, Bill."

"You think we are, too."

"Not quite so much as you evidently do. I'll admit I'm short of one vital fact."

"What's that?"

"How did the cyanide get into Jimmy Cleveland's mouth? I've a feeling that if I could discover that . . ."

"I know," replied Green. "I've been thinking about it."

"Did you come to any conclusion?"

"Only that he somehow got it on his hands and then shoved his fingers in his mouth to pick a strand of breakfast bacon from between two of his teeth, or something like that." He stooped to fondle a chocolate-coloured dog, of no one obvious make, which had been skittering about the beach all day.

Masters said: "I think you'll not be far wrong with that idea, Bill."

"But?"

"The trouble is we're faced with the problem of discovering how the cyanide got on his hands in the first place."

"I know." Green stooped to pick up a pebble. The dog bounced around him expectantly. Green tossed it into the wavelets lapping the shore. "That little thing has been rushing up and down all day. He's waiting for his master who is out on the water. He just . . . ouch! You little perisher!" The dog had come out of the water, dropped a stone at Green's feet and had then shaken itself, spraying him with droplets. The dog waited expectantly, eyeing Green. "That's not the pebble I threw in," Green said to it. "Mine was a red and white one. That's grey." The dog didn't care. It wagged its tail as much as to ask: 'What's all the fuss about? A stone is a stone, of whatever colour. The game's the thing, so throw another one for me.'

Green stooped again to pick up the stone the dog had brought ashore. "The trouble with you, feller, is that there are so many pebbles out there, you don't know which one to pick up." The dog pranced in anticipation. "Just like us with clues, in fact." He lobbed the stone and the dog lolloped into the water. "We don't know what's what and which to seize on."

To Green's great surprise, he felt Masters grasp his upper arm in a grip of great strength. He looked round at the DCS. "Something, George?" he asked quietly.

"Yes, Bill, thanks to you."

Green remained quiet. Masters let go his arm and looked about him. At last he spied a short stick at the water's edge. He picked it up and handed it to Green who had just dodged a second shower from the returning dog. "Try him with that, Bill."

Wordlessly, Green took the stick and threw it into the water. In a moment the dog was back with it in his mouth.

"He got the right one that time, Bill."

"Yes."

"In fact he'd get the right one every time if you continued to use the stick instead of the pebble."

"So?"

"Impregnate it with cyanide . . ."

"And I'd be sure to kill him."

"That's right."

"Meaning we've got to find something like the stick a dog fetches that a sailor is certain to stick in his mouth . . . come off it, George. What are grown-up blokes going to shove in their mouths? Dummies?"

Masters shook his head. "Listen, Bill. This is my idea, sparked by your game with that dog. Thank heaven you're a dog-lover."

130

"I'm not. Not particularly, that is. It's just that Nel was so appealing when I first saw her. Still is, I suppose. This little chap is a sort of stand-in for her. The liking overflowed, if you like."

"No matter. This is the idea."

Masters spoke for several minutes, just long enough for Green to smoke one cigarette. When he came to the end, he asked: "What do you think, Bill?"

Green ground the cigarette butt into the sand. "I'd say it's got to be right, George, if you can confirm it tomorrow morning when you go out to watch the race."

"Are you happy to proceed as though I am right before I can confirm it?"

"We'd be fools not to."

"Then can I ask you to keep your eyes open, down here, as they come in? I know some are already ashore, but the vast majority are only just rounding the end of the quay. I'll send whoever I can find to join you. If I can get Berger, I'll send him down with the camera."

"Doris has got one of those little instant colour things. Ask her to lend it and any spare packs she's got to Tip."

"Right. I'll station myself near the ramp up to the boat. Tip can operate there. They have to queue up at that point, so she can act the part of an ordinary holidaymaker taking snaps."

"Right, George, get weaving, and let's wrap this up."

"Yes, sir, Bill."

"You know what I mean."

"Of course. Keep your eyes skinned. Don't get too taken up with the dog."

As the craft arrived at the water's edge, the Beach Master's crew of youths trundled the launching trolleys down from where they had been parked and, usually with the help of the crews, manoeuvred the flimsy vehicles under the keels of the craft which were being kept just afloat until this operation was completed. Then the trolleys and their burdens were hauled out. As Masters had predicted, after the first few had come home singly, the greater proportion of the fleet arrived almost together. Helms and crew members had to stand off twenty or thirty yards to await their turn to beach. Spinnakers were stowed and mainsails lowered, while the foresails were left up to give the little craft just enough power to answer to their helms and prevent a log jam of bumping and grinding hulls.

Green, with Berger, stood just far enough away from the scene of operations to avoid being a nuisance to the beach party. There were two hauling out points where the heavy black rubber treading had been run down into the water. Green stationed himself between them, just at the point where they altered direction through 90 degrees to head for the ramp up to the dinghy park.

"That one, lad," grunted Green to Berger. "Don't make it obvious. I want full face of the chap in the navy blue shirt."

"Why?"

"Never mind why. Get it. Full face of that one chap, and don't make it obvious that's your object. You're just taking snaps. Got it?"

Berger was a trained photograher. He could operate a zoom lens in his sleep. He decided on two shots each time.

"There's another I want, son. The bloke with the yellow nylon cover-alls. Face only. Big as you can get him."

"His hat's over his eyes."

"Never mind. Get the rest of his physog."

The camera clicked on. Green selected four faces. Then there was a lull, and finally, to Berger's surprise, no more shots to be taken.

"Come along, lad," said Green. "We're shifting."

"Where to?"

"First, off to have a word with his nibs at the ramp."

The excellent organization of the Cullermouth Club was very much in evidence at the ramp. Here, two black rubber hoses had been attached to outside taps, and the queuing crews waited their turn to hose down. The water washing off the hulls sank immediately into the dry, powdery sand, so there was no build-up of mud or puddles. But as the boats went up the ramp, the final drops dripping from the keels were wetting the black rubber strips. This, combined with the light dusting of sand already covering them, had made the slope slippery, if not actually greasy. But this had been foreseen. The rubber strips had been pushed together in the middle of the ramp to take the trolley wheels. This left eighteen inches or so of wooden sleepers, laid horizontally, on each side. As a dinghy got to the bottom of the ramp, two heavy ropes with loops at the end were snaked down to the crews. The loops were slipped over the bars of the trolley's lifting handles. Helm and crew, one each side, lifted the handles. A group of the Beach Master's team took the strain on the ropes. Then the craft went up at a run, crew and helm just managing to keep their feet on the sleepers at the sides.

Although done with great despatch, it was still a slow business. Masters was pleased about that. Hovering around the washdown and the foot of the ramp, with Tip in attendance, he was able to choose his subjects quite carefully. Tip could then take her time over her shots, waiting carefully until she could get the sun behind her and shining full on the faces she was snapping. Masters was sure it aroused no suspicion. Tip acted just like any ordinary seaside picture-taker, and the crews were so involved with their own business that it was doubtful whether any of them paid her any attention.

Green approached Masters and drew him aside.

"We've come to the end down there, George. You've still got some to come through, but I've got a feeling we missed most of them."

"How come, Bill?"

"I reckon for the most part they'd be the ones who came in at the beginning. The keen types. The better sailors, if you like."

"Ah! I see your point, Bill."

"I think I'll go into the Race Office and get the names of the first six or eight—names of boats, I mean—then Berger and I could wander around up top and see if I'm right."

"Good idea, Bill. But send Berger into the office for the names. You go up and scout around until he joins you. You could strike oil better the fewer boats there are up there."

Green grunted assent and then returned to where Berger waited.

Green trudged through the Wet Bar and up the short flight of concrete steps to reach the dinghy park. The bar was doing a thriving trade, and Stan was too busy to notice the detective wending his way through the collection of motley-dressed sailors all holding long drinks and gabbling away about the day's events out on the water. He had to stand aside at the steps to allow more through, and when he got up on the bank he stopped to stare in amazement. Chaos! Some of the craft had been pulled out of line and were careened over while people did things to mastheads or centre-boards. Tool boxes and bags were open everywhere. Some were sawing, some filing, some sandpapering. There were even some sewing with large needles and sailmaker's palms. Others were standing with large tankards in their hands, watching their colleagues work. Wives and girlfriends had arrived to talk animatedly or to lie out in sundresses while their menfolk toiled. The men seemed to have divested themselves of wet suits or dry suits and now wore nothing above the waist. Overalls slipped off shoulders and tied by the arms round the midriff, shorts, bathing-trunks, tattered denims . . . Green guessed there was as big a variety of dress, including footwear, as one could possibly meet in one place. And an incessant gabble of tongues, punctuated by the sounds of the various jobs that were being undertaken to repair the ravages of the day and in preparation for the big event later in the week.

Green passed between two boats that were still on their trailers and slowly walked along the line which was, as yet, far from complete. He tried to select those which looked as if they had been out of the water the longest and to scrutinize their crews to see whether they had passed him whilst he and Berger had been at the water's edge.

He felt quite satisfied with the idea to come up here to have a look at the early finishers. He reckoned he had another three clients at least. Berger found him standing near the single-rail fence that separated the boat park from the drop down into the moat.

"Nine of them got in before the mob," said Berger. The first was *Fascinating Rhythm* and that's parked at berth number seventeen. *Mare's Tail* number eleven, was second. Then came *Crossbow* number forty two, *Summer Sail* number forty, *Pitch an' Toss* number three, *Swell Party* twenty three, *Horizontal Heavyweight* number six, *Festina Lente* number thirty, *Water Sprite* number . . ."

"That's enough," growled Green. "*Water Sprite* was our first one. So we'll take the other eight. Here, give me that list and we'll do them as we come to them. I don't want to be trudging from end to end of this hump just to take them in order."

It was as Green had remarked on his earlier tour. Three out of the first eight were clients for Berger's camera. The sergeant made great play of just taking fun shots, but he did a professional job, as Green knew he would.

"You'll have to get back to the local nick to get that lot developed and printed. We shall want them by tomorrow morning at the latest."

Berger looked about him. "I've got three left," he said. "How about a nice picture of you in your braces?" Green, who was wearing a pair of decent grey slacks and a linen bush-shirt, specially tailored for him so that it had four patch-pockets in which to carry the impedimenta he needed for day-to-day existence, aimed a playful kick at him.

"Seriously though?" queried Berger, dodging neatly.

"Just take three long shots along this line," grunted Green. "Start at one end and then move up a third of the way and so on."

"What use will that be?"

"I don't know lad. But if nothing else it will illustrate your plan."

Berger nodded and set off to take the shots. Green wandered along towards the top of the ramp up to the dinghy park, in the hope of finding Masters.

*

135

"All done," said Masters quietly. "Now we've got quite a bit to do, Bill. Where's Berger?"

"He'll be along in a minute."

"Good. I want to talk to him and Tip."

"Did the lass get some good shots?"

"Excellent." Masters handed over a pile of the self-printing snaps. "Have a look."

Green took them and studied each in turn. "They duplicate some of ours, of course, but they're good."

"I think so. I want those people identifying."

"You won't get Berger's before the morning."

"We should do. There are plenty of photographic shops that will develop and print inside an hour, or two hours at the most. He can ask Ashley or Sandy for an address and get them done."

Berger arrived and was told what was required of him.

"Right, Chief. I've made a bit of a hit with the girl in the Race Office. She'll be able to identify some of these. And, incidentally, Chief, she has invited me to the barbecue tonight."

"Good. Take Tip along with you."

"Have a heart, Chief."

"I want her there. You and she will, by then, have a list of names. Talking of which . . ."

"I've got them, Chief. Typed out."

"What?" demanded Green.

"Names of people with vans and tents," said Berger off-handedly. "The Chief thought we ought to have them."

"Did he!"

"So I'll get along, Chief. It'll probably be five before I have the prints, so I'll see you at the local nick, shall I?"

"Yes. Take the local car. Leave ours."

"You've got the keys, Chief."

"So I have. Right, get off now."

Green looked at the disarray of dinghies. "What now, George?"

"We'll have a word with the chap whose boat is just this side of Martin's. *Slowcoach*, it's called. The owner is Dennis Goldie."

"Any particular reason?"

"I think so. It should be obvious as we talk."

"Wait a minute! He's the chap who lost a rope."

"That's him."

Masters and Green pretended they had gone along to examine Martin's *Spearhead*. They tested the cover lashings and then Masters turned to the man working not more than four feet away. "Good afternoon, Mr Goldie. Any news of your missing mainsheet?"

Goldie straightened up. "Not a word. I didn't expect there would be."

"Don't give up hope yet. When exactly did you miss it?"

"This morning, otherwise I wouldn't have had to send Len Goatcher into town to buy a new one."

"So it was there last evening when you snugged down?"

Goldie stared at him for a moment. "Well, now you come to mention it, I can't be sure."

"No?"

"I didn't sail yesterday."

"May I ask why not?"

"Because I was away on business."

"Do you live close by?"

"No."

Masters felt he was making too little headway on this tack. "So when did you last see your mainsheet?"

"On Sunday, about this time."

"I see. Your crew? Mr Goatcher, did you say his name was? Wasn't he here yesterday, either?"

"When he knew I wouldn't be sailing he decided not to come down either. He went sightseeing."

"I see. So your rope could have disappeared at any time between four on Sunday afternoon and, say, eight o'clock this morning?"

"Give or take half-an-hour each way, yes."

"I see. Well, we shall keep our eyes and ears open in the hope of finding your mainsheet."

"A fat chance of your finding it."

"Maybe, but you never know. There have been one or two other incidents concerning boat tackle. We have them in mind. If we turn anything up about any one of them it could give us a lead on the others. By the way, where is Mr Goatcher? I thought it was the duty of every good crew to lend a helping hand with making everything shipshape."

"He's gone to get some plasters for blisters."

"For his hands?"

"No, mine. This new rope is a bit too new and stiff for comfort at the moment. It will soften down."

"I see. But he has escaped, has he?"

"Blisters? Oh, yes. He's getting drinks as well."

Masters and Green nodded farewell and made for the clubhouse.

"I think we should be making tracks for the local nick, George."

Masters, in deep thought, nodded agreement.

"Do you want me to see if I can spot Tip?"

"What? Sorry Bill. Yes, if you can see her . . . we'd better be going."

Green raised his eyes to heaven and grimaced. By that time, Masters was again deep in thought.

They were at the Wearbay police station.

"What about Mr Pedder, Chief?" asked Finch.

"Has he rung yet?"

"No."

"Then wait until he does, or at least until after our chat."

"Are you expecting to have something concrete to report to him then?"

"No. But I think I shall be in a better position to reassure him that we are making progress. And I'm afraid assurances will be all he will get at this stage."

"That should be enough for him. With your reputation, I mean, Chief."

"Very kind of you to say so, Sandy, but we're not home yet.

And by the way, you had a man on guard at Martin's boat, didn't you?"

"Forensic and scene-of-crime said it wasn't necessary as they'd finished with it, but I kept one there all the same. Until this morning, that is, then I thought that with all of us there, and in view of what I'd been told, it was no longer necessary. So I withdrew the guard."

"Please send a man down now. Without delay. I just had enough of my wits about me before we left Abbot's Haven to post Tip at the boat until relieved."

"You think it will be interfered with?"

"I think there is every likelihood, once the coast is clear."

Sandy Finch scratched an ear. "You think we have got close enough to cause some reaction?"

Masters looked somewhat grim-faced. "As to that, I can't say specifically. But I know I have blundered in not having that dinghy guarded ever since my arrival at Abbot's Haven early this morning."

"Meaning I should have disregarded what the forensic people said and had the dinghy brought in here?" Finch sounded angry at Masters' implied criticism and his voice had hardened in consequence.

"Yes and no. Yes, you should have guarded the boat despite what forensic said, and no, you shouldn't have removed it."

"Why on earth not?"

"Because the position it occupies could be important."

"I wasn't to know that."

"I am not saying you should, so don't blast Ashley Head for failing to do what I failed to do myself, and don't get steamed up yourself. Everybody makes mistakes. Yours is less reprehensible than most because you were acting on information given you by the scene-of-crime experts. All I'm asking is that both of us—you and I—should learn from our mistakes, or at least repair them. Now, can we please forget this incident, and will you arrange for the boat to be guarded until further notice?"

Finch shook his head in bewilderment and turned away.

Green said quietly to Masters, "I should have made sure it was guarded, George. It's my responsibility, that sort of thing, as your number two."

"Yours, Bill. Mine. Finch's and Head's. We slipped up. I hope we've not been too remiss and that we've managed to bolt the door before the horse bolted."

Green grunted, whether in agreement or in doubt as to the likelihood of the steps that had now been taken being successful was not clear. "Shall I round people up?"

"Muster as soon as Tip and Berger appear, please, Bill."

"There's Ashley now."

"Good. I'd like a word with him."

"Going to blast him, are you, in spite of telling Sandy not to?"

Masters grinned. "Far from it. Is he a married man, by the way?"

"I don't know, but I'd have said not. His taste in seaside-wear somehow smacks of bachelordom to me, but I could have misread the signs."

"Call him over then, Bill, please."

Head came across. "Mr Green said you wanted a word, Chief."

"Yes, please. Shall we get off this landing and go into your office? Lord knows what we're standing about out here for."

"I stopped here," said Green who had followed Head towards Masters, "because it's the coolest place. Two windows open and opposite each other and the breath of a draft blowing through."

"Was it about not posting a guard on the boat, Chief? Sandy's mentioned it to me and . . ." He followed Masters into the office.

"No, not that. Are you married, Ashley?"

"Not so's you'd notice, Chief."

"Good. Then you won't mind taking Tip along to the barbecue at the club tonight."

Head grinned. "I certainly won't mind, but I've never had senior officers arranging dates for me before."

"It's in the line of duty, lad," grunted Green.

140

"Pity. But whatever."

"We'll tell you all about it when Tip gets here." Masters took the desk seat. "Make sure we've got enough chairs, Ashley, please."

Masters spoke for some time when all his team had assembled. There was a lot to pull together. Then he started asking questions.

He turned to Berger first.

"I asked you to discover who owned a certain caravan."

"Yes, Chief. It is owned by Len Goatcher."

"So presumably the woman I saw there was Mrs Goatcher."

"I expect so, Chief. Mrs Goatcher is up here with her husband. Her name is Avril."

"But the man I saw leaving the van in a clandestine fashion, after kissing Mrs Goatcher at the door, could not have been Mr Goatcher. He was out on the water, crewing for Denis Goldie in *Slowcoach*. At the same time I saw them, no boat had returned, and Goldie came back, as I remember, well down the fleet."

"That's right, Chief," said Tip. "*Slowcoach* was one of the boats I photographed towards the end of the time we were at the ramp."

"Thank you. I've spoken to Goldie this afternoon, but I didn't meet Goatcher, but it was presumably his face you snapped."

"That's right." Tip shuffled her photographs before finally selecting one. "This is Len Goatcher, Chief."

"Thank you. Will everybody take a look, because I think Goatcher could be of interest to us. As, indeed are all the people whose faces appear on the photographs. How many are there all told, Bill?"

"We duplicated quite a lot. About eleven, I think."

"Thank you. We're all interested in all of them, because I think that among those eleven men is the one whom our murderer intended to kill."

There was a moment of stunned silence before Sandy Finch asked, "Are you now sure that Jimmy Cleveland was killed by mistake?"

"I said I think the victim is among the eleven, Sandy. But my belief is so strong that I want an eye kept on each of them, to decide why they should have been singled out for attack. There could be some facet of their behaviour which has caused it. So, tonight, there is a barbecue on the beach. Sergeant Berger is attending it with the girl from the Race Office. I've asked Ashley and Tip to attend also. So there will be three pairs of eyes on the job. I want all three of you to memorize those eleven faces and to observe exactly what goes on."

"Shouldn't we increase the number of watchers, Chief?" asked Finch.

"I think not, Sandy, otherwise you, Bill and I would attend. My fear would be that if we swamp the place with coppers, the people there may become so circumspect that we shall have wasted our time and our opportunity. However, I am willing to change my decision if you and Bill both consider I should do so."

Green held back to allow Finch to reply. "On balance, I think you're probably right, Chief, but we could miss something. Where would we be then?"

"Not entirely lost, I hope." He turned to Green. "What do you think, Bill?"

"We don't want to fall over each others' feet."

"Meaning you think the three should be enough?"

Green nodded. "Particularly if you've got other ways of arriving at the answer."

"I think we might have. But to continue with the photographs. I want those eleven faces identifying, to-night, please. By tomorrow morning, Ashley, I want you to be able to mark them off on the names on Berger's chart."

"Right, Chief."

"Sandy, you have two jobs to do on the chart. If Ashley uses a yellow marker, I'd like you to use a pink one, for all the people on your list who have been to the following foreign countries within the last year." Masters handed over the list he had compiled from the *Pharmacopoeia*. Finch looked at it

142

with some dismay. "I'm certain not all these places figure on my list, Chief."

"Have you covered everybody for foreign travel?"

"Not quite. There's about half a dozen I'll have to ask outright."

"If you have to, but I'd rather you got the information by indirect means if you can."

"I'll see what I can do. If you don't mind me going to the barbecue, that is."

"Go, by all means, if you feel it will help. And if you do go, kill two birds with one stone and co-operate with Ashley and the others in keeping an eye not only on the eleven, but on Mrs Avril Goatcher, too, and another woman called Connie Akers."

"Will do, Chief."

"Thank you. Now, your second chore. Here is a list of all the jobs and processes which can legitimately use cyanide. Compare those with your list of occupations, and use pale blue to mark on the chart any of them that could conceivably come in contact with cyanide."

"Conceivably?"

"Yes. All those who could be directly involved, and those who might be involved. What I mean is, cyanide is used in photographic processing. If you've got a chap who works in one of the big film-processing plants, you've got a direct contact. If you've got a man who clips films for studio rushes or who works in film archives or something of the sort, include him, because though he may not need to use cyanide himself, he could be in a position to know somebody who does."

Finch nodded to show he understood. "You're hoping that yellow, pink and blue are all going to appear beside at least one name?"

"That could be a little too much to hope for, but I certainly hope we're going to narrow the field this way. All that by tomorrow morning, please, gentlemen."

"What time, Chief?"

"The earlier the better. Certainly before Ashley and I take

143

our trip out to the fleet. And in that connection, Ashley, I'd like you to arrange for Harry Martin to accompany us."

"If I don't see him at the barbecue, Chief, I'll see him at his hotel. Ready to go off at nine-thirty?"

"Yes, please. With binoculars."

There was a little pause while they all looked expectantly at Masters who frowned in concentration for a moment or two before continuing.

"I should like to know the identity of the man who visited Mrs Goatcher's van this afternoon."

"He's obviously not a sailor, Chief."

"Quite, Ashley, but I have a sneaking suspicion you might know him. He was heavily built, and though I was some distance away I think I could say he was expensively dressed. On the flashy side, rather. Mid-blue slacks; shirt something like apricot in colour; shoes—real shoes, not trainers or anything of that sort—brown ones that from where I was sitting, looked as if they could be of very soft leather, yet they shone. Rather low heels, I fancy. Oh, and a watch on a yellow metal bracelet and wrap-around sunglasses. That's about as much as I can tell you."

"Hair colour, Chief?"

"Sorry. Indefinite is all I can say to that, but there wasn't a lot of it, if my memory is correct. I don't mean by that that he was bald, just that his hair was trimmed, styled rather more neatly than some are these days."

"Age?"

"No close guess, but I'll stick my neck out and say between thirty and forty. He definitely didn't move like a youngster, but he was pretty agile at climbing the bank behind the van and ducking out of sight."

"You seem to be giving a description that could fit Maurice Hunt, the furnisher," said Head. "Not exactly, of course. Or I'd have said not. But I don't know him all that well."

"I thought you might say that." Masters turned to Green. "While Ashley and I are at sea tomorrow morning, Bill, will you and Tip try to establish whether the description I've just given you does fit Maurice Hunt? You'll have a car for getting about in, and I expect your friend Stan might recognize my memory picture. Then, perhaps, you might visit the camp site and see if anybody there saw this character, when he arrived, how often he's been there and so on."

"We'll manage that," said Green, turning to Tip. "Won't we, petal?"

"You and I together can tackle anything. And I'll look out for him tonight, too."

"That's my girl."

"Thank you, all," said Masters. "I know that I've thrown a lot of stuff at you, and that it is terribly disjointed. But I feel we've got most of what we want now. There are a few more bits and pieces to worry over, but I shall let you have those tomorrow morning. Chiefly for you, Sandy, and you, Berger."

"The man on duty at the boat, Chief?" asked Finch. "Anything for him?"

"The craft is not to be touched by anybody. To that end, it is to be patrolled closely every second of the time. Warn your man not to stand still anywhere for more than a few seconds, because anybody intent on doing so could crawl-approach quite easily in the shadows of the other craft. To reach up and put a hand under the cover would be child's play if the watcher were standing a few yards away on the other side of the craft."

"I'll make sure he knows it all when I see him tonight. In fact, I'll post two of them turn-and-turn-about and make sure the Panda patrol calls on them every hour as well."

"Thank you. That will do very well, because the watch can be completely overt—nothing clandestine about it."

"Let's hope we're not too late to prevent whatever it is you're worried about."

"Evidence, chum," said Green, getting to his feet and stretching. "Is that it, George?"

"Yes, thank you. We will meet for breakfast at the club at half-past-seven."

As the meeting broke up, Masters said to Finch: "I'll call Mr

145

Pedder, now. Bill, I'll drive us home in the Yard car. Berger and Tip can use the one Ashley supplied."

"I think that's laid on."

"Good. Give me a few minutes to ring Pedder."

"Give him my love."

"With pleasure." Masters picked up the phone and asked for a connection to the Nortown HQ.

Chapter 5

MASTERS WAS THOUGHTFUL as he drove the big Rover back
to Stanhope. Green, recognizing the signs, said nothing
except to give the occasional direction from the map he was
reading. Masters accepted—and obeyed—these instructions in silence. Green, sitting in what, for him, was the
unaccustomed front seat, made sure the belt was at its tightest
by frequent tests of the tension, and smoked cigarette after
cigarette in his effort to subdue the paranoic fear he always
had when in a car, but particularly when sitting in any place
other than at the nearside rear. Reading the map helped, too.
Masters didn't need the instructions given, but maps were
one of Green's great loves. He would pore over them out of
sheer enjoyment and he could interpret them skilfully. For
this reason, and the fact that such an activity helped to occupy
Green's mind and so lessened his fear of heavy traffic,
Masters made no objections to the unnecessary instructions
that interrupted his flow of thought. It was only after they
had climbed the hill outside Crook and were heading
towards Wolsingham and Green said, "Just a few miles now,
George. Straight on as you go", that Masters murmured his
thanks for the help given. The traffic had now lessened
considerably and Green closed the atlas.

"Let's have it, then, chum."

"My thoughts?"

"What else? You've been as quiet as a clam with toothache
ever since we got into this barouche. Did Alf Pedder say
something you didn't like?"

Masters grinned. "No, in fact he was strangely docile and
co-operative."

"Co-operative? What about? He's the sleeping partner in

this firm. What is there for him to co-operate about?"

The road ahead was almost clear. Just one distant car approaching them. Masters lowered the visor against the now lowering sun before replying.

"Has it occurred to you, Bill, that there is one person who could be an important witness whom we haven't seen, or even mentioned as yet?"

"One?" snorted Green. "There are scads of them. There's the American quack for one. His daughter for another. The rescue people who brought the lad ashore. The crews of the dinghies closest to *Spearhead* in the race. And quite a few more I could mention, if you want me to."

"We've only been on the job for about twenty-four hours from first mention," complained Masters mildly.

"I know that." Green lit another cigarette. "But you did ask. If you don't want me to list our shortcomings, you should be a bit more specific with your questions."

This time Masters laughed.

"Go on," grunted Green. "Who is it?"

"Jimmy Cleveland's girlfriend, Janet."

"She wasn't even up here, so how can she be involved?"

"Directly? Not at all, one would suppose, but I've got a feeling we ought to talk to her. To her, rather than to Matt, I mean."

Green considered this point for a moment. "To get to know young Jimmy's state of mind in the past few weeks? I don't see how that can be significant if we're satisfied he didn't commit suicide. I know the girl would be closer to him down in London than Matt and Philippa would, because she's been in his company lately where they haven't. And you know all this as well as I do, so you've got some other bee in your bonnet, George. Does that mean you're setting out for New Malden?"

"No. I told Alf Pedder I wanted to see her and he told me she has come up here to comfort Matt and Philippa."

"I reckon it's real nice of a young lass to do that. The house can't be a very cheerful place to visit, but I'll bet Philippa is grateful to her."

148

"I agree," said Masters, as they ran into the outskirts of Stanhope.

"So when and where do we see her?"

"Here, tonight."

"Here? At the cottage?"

"Yes. Alf says he'll bring her over personally. I think he saw the opportunity to come and discuss things with us himself, so he offered to drive her here."

"You mean he's like a cat on hot bricks," snorted Green.

"That's it. He's anxious for news—more than I could give him over the phone, I mean—but he's being sensible enough to leave things to us and not to interfere unduly."

"What time? After we've had chance to have our grub, I hope?"

"Nine-ish."

"Fair enough. It's not half-past-seven yet and if the girls have been on the ball in the kitchen . . . you know, George, it seems years ago since I had that bully sandwich for lunch."

The car took the hairpin bend out of the little market place and then turned right-handed down the gently curving slope to the cottage.

"No Nel," said Green.

"She's probably gone home for a proper supper. She doesn't seem to have had much except ginger biscuits for a day or two."

"I know," said Green gloomily. "And now, just when I expect Wanda's got me a packet of Ovals for her, she's deserted us."

"Nonsense, Bill. How can you possibly say Nel's deserted you? As like as not she'll be back as soon as she can get out of her own house—if that's where she's gone."

Masters switched off the engine and undid his seat belt. Wanda appeared at the cottage door. "I haven't seen Nel, William. She wasn't here when we got home."

Masters kissed her. "Bill thinks Nel has deserted us."

Wanda turned to Green. "Oh, I do hope not, William. She's become quite one of the family."

"She's probably where she ought to be," said Masters, "and

149

that's where she belongs. In her own home. But to cheer Bill up I'll get him a stiff drink before supper."

"You'd better go and get into your best glad rags," Green said to Doris as he sat down with his drink. "We've got company coming."

"Company? Who? Oh, you mean Sergeant Berger and Tip."

"Sergeant!" said her husband snootily. "No less a person than a Chief Constable."

"What? You're pulling my leg, Bill Green."

"Honest truth, love. After supper. So let's be having it. George and I will want to change, too."

"What into?"

"Our second-best drinking suits, of course."

Wanda asked: "Is Mr Pedder really coming, George?"

Masters nodded. "He's bringing Jimmy Cleveland's girl-friend to see us. She's come up here to be with Matt and Philippa, and I want to see her."

"You think it would be better to talk to her in a family atmosphere rather than at the police station in the village?"

"Yes. And I didn't think I could go to the Clevelands' house to interview her."

"Quite right. She'll be happier here. Supper will be ready quite soon, but we're having a savoury custard and we couldn't start to cook that until you got here."

"Savoury custard?" snorted Green. "That's for afters, I hope."

"For afters, starters and middlers," retorted his wife. "There's only one course."

Green turned to Masters. "We needn't have bothered, George. We could have gone to that pub at Fir Tree . . ."

"Greedy guts," said Doris. "You just don't deserve all the care and attention Wanda's put into preparing this meal."

"I can't eat care and attention."

"Pig," snorted his wife, and left the sitting room to join Wanda in the kitchen.

In the event, even Green was satisfied with the savoury

custard and the deep pizza that accompanied it with buttered new potatoes and green beans.

"After that," he sighed as he finished, "I'll forgive you the half truths—no, the quarter truths—you told me earlier on, love." He looked across at Masters. "I suppose that's what we've been getting all day, isn't it? Quarter truths?"

"We've only been grasping about a quarter," agreed Masters. "But just as you eventually got the full helping, I have high hopes that we shall soon have an equally satisfying repast."

Wanda said: "You're beginning to get the feel of the problem, darling?"

"I think that describes it exactly."

Doris said: "I don't think I understand that bit, George."

"Sorry if I was being obscure, Doris. The best way I can think of describing it is to imagine an avid and successful solver of the crossword puzzle in his daily paper who is suddenly faced with the fact that the paper has changed the man who sets the puzzle. The new poser puts his clues in so different a manner that our man is no longer a successful solver. At least, not immediately. But after a few days he begins to think in the same way as the new poser and gradually begins to get the hang of the clues until he is once more successful."

"You mean this is a really new sort of puzzle for you?"

"In several respects, yes. The boy died very, very quickly, two miles out at sea, and virtually alone. That would not be quite so much of a poser if he had eaten or drunk something. But he didn't, so first of all, we've got to decide how he did ingest the poison. Then where did it come from, who provided it and why? And all in the middle of a sailing jamboree which is a totally different environment from anything we've ever met before. In other words, whoever has set this puzzle for us has written the clues in a different fashion. Fortunately, as with a crossword puzzle where anagrams are anagrams, no matter who writes the clues, one of the usual motives will apply. Human greed, jealousy, sex or what have you."

Doris looked at him, wide-eyed. "And does Bill help with all this? Really help? The thinking, I mean? I know he can do the routine well enough . . ."

Masters grinned. "With your old man sitting here, I'll not give you a direct answer to that, but I should remind you that over the past few years I've fought tooth and nail against all manner of opposition to keep him with me, and my own superiors value his services so much that they are prepared to keep him on long after normal retirement age at a time when others are being asked to go early."

"I know," said Doris simply. "And it's very nice, too. But I've always found it so hard to believe. Really believe, I mean."

"There you are," growled Green, embarrassed by the conversation.

"There I am what?" asked Doris.

Wanda intervened. "I'm sure I'm not as good at producing apt quotations as you are, William, but I think I can offer you just a little one at this particular moment." Wanda raised her glass. "It was Alexander Pope, I think, who wrote, 'Worth makes the man, and want of it the fellow'."

Masters applauded. Doris was bright-eyed and her husband more embarrassed than ever.

It was just after nine-twenty when Pedder arrived. With him came his wife, Mary, and Janet, Jimmy Cleveland's girl-friend.

"Had to go to the local nick to get directions for finding you," said Pedder, "and they didn't even know who I was."

His wife smiled and, behind her husband's back, winked at Masters. Mary Pedder had entertained Masters and Green some months before, but neither she nor her husband had met Doris and Wanda. And that, she declared, was one of the main reasons for suggesting she should accompany Janet over to Stanhope.

"Now Judder," said Pedder, "I'd like a private word with you and Bill, before you talk to Janet."

"Guessed you would, Alf," said Green. "But we've not got

152

much room here, so Wanda and Doris were going to sit in the kitchen while we had a word in the sitting room."

"Janet and I will join you," said Mary Pedder to Wanda. "If that's all right?"

"We've got four dining chairs round the table," said Wanda, "a litre of plonk and lots of glasses. Alternatively, we've got coffee granules, cups and an electric kettle."

"The plonk sounds lovely. Is that all right for you, Janet?"

The girl smiled. "Perfect, thank you. I feel I could do with a . . . a bit of a boost, and a glass of wine would be marvellous."

When the three men were seated in the sitting room, Pedder led off by saying, "You've told me a good bit about your activities already, George, but you haven't told me any of the thinking behind it. I know better than to suppose that what you've been doing has no apparent purpose, but I'm nonetheless curious to know what end you're working to."

"I understand that, Alf, and there are a number of things I feel I can tell you. For instance, Bill and I think we know how the poison was administered, but we shall have to wait until tomorrow to prove it beyond doubt."

"Tell me," said Pedder.

Masters did so. The explanation took less than five minutes. At the end of it, Pedder put down the drink he had been holding and stared for a moment before saying, "It beats me how you do it, Judder."

"Blame it on Bill," said Masters.

Pedder faced Green. "Nothing to do with me," said Green. "It was Nel."

"Who in heaven's name is Nel?" demanded the CC.

"A sheepdog—or a sheepbitch, rather," answered Green.

"All right, all right. I should know better than to ask you a lot of questions. But you know how the cyanide was administered. And that's a hell of a lot. What else?"

"It wasn't intended for young Cleveland—in our opinion," replied Masters.

"Oh, no," groaned Pedder. "Poor old bloody Matt! And Philippa! To know some murdering bastard killed their boy by mistake."

"I said that is our belief. We hope to confirm that shortly."

"By asking another bitch for its opinion?"

"I would hardly refer to Janet in that way, Alf, but I'm hoping she can help us to confirm it. You'll be here when we talk to her, so there's no need for me to say more now."

Pedder grimaced. "Where did the cyanide come from?"

"We don't know—yet. We've taken certain steps towards finding out, of course."

"I'll bet you have. And that leaves motive. I suppose we have to find one?"

"In this case, Alf, yes. Without it, we'll never discover Chummy, and it's a tangled skein of relationships we've got to unravel."

"In what way?"

Again Masters spoke for about five minutes. When he stopped, Pedder said, "There's either somebody who's infernally clever behind all this, or else he's had the luck of the devil."

"A bit of both," said Green.

"He's going to take some winkling out."

"Yes," said Masters.

"Is that all you've got to say, Judder? Yes?"

"What more is there?"

"You must have some inkling."

Masters shook his head. "I mustn't try to guess at this stage, Alf. If I were to do so, I could obfuscate the issue in my own mind which I am striving desperately to keep open."

"And that's as good a way of telling me to mind my own business as any I've heard in years."

Masters smiled. "It could appear that way, but I assure you it isn't. I think I've got nearly all the pieces of the jigsaw, but it's one of those with an overall indeterminate colour with no obvious delineation anywhere in it. In other words, I've got to test every piece, and that's a tedious job."

Pedder drained his glass. "But at least you've got all the straight-edge pieces lined up?"

"The framework, yes," admitted Masters, "but for the build-up, I've got to start guessing—picking bits out at

154

random, if you like, just to get a start."

"That's right, Alf," grunted Green. "For instance, this conversation George is going to have with this little lass, Janet, is a bit of a shot in the dark. If she provides the answers to confirm what he suspects, well then, we're away. If she doesn't, we have to start again."

"To find a new theory?"

"A modified one," said Masters, "because I'm pretty sure we're on the right track."

"In that case," said Pedder, getting to his feet, "the sooner we have the girlie in, the better. I'll fetch her."

"And I'll top up your glass while you're away," said Green.

"Make it a weak one. I'm driving, remember."

Masters, standing as the girl came into the room, said, "Please sit down, Miss Galliford. That is right, isn't it?"

"Galliford? Yes."

She was a handsome girl, simply-dressed in a white broderie anglaise blouse and a full cotton skirt in canary yellow. Her legs were bare and she wore little yellow sandals to match the skirt. Her features were strong—a straight nose, firm chin and big dark eyes. Masters noticed that though she wore a smudge of eye shadow, the eyebrows were dark, slightly heavy, and owed nothing to make-up. She wore her dark hair shoulder length. It shone cleanly, tumbling in natural waves that were highlighted in the light of the ceiling lamp that was now switched on.

"Call her Janet," said Pedder, picking up his glass. "More friendly than your southern formality, George."

"Yes, please," said the girl, setting down the half-glass of white wine she had brought in with her from the kitchen. "Mr and Mrs Cleveland have been telling me about you. They asked me to remember them to you and Mr Green, and to say . . ."—she smiled sadly—". . . that they think none of us could be in better hands."

Green cleared his throat, not displeased by the comment or at the thought that at such a time Matt and Philippa should send a greeting, but embarrassed by the sentiments, nonetheless. Masters merely said, "It is very kind of them to say that. Now, Janet . . ."

The girl sat up a little straighter.

"How long had you known Jimmy?"

"Just to say hello to, for nearly a year. Ever since he came down to New Malden and joined the sailing club."

"But you became much closer friends, didn't you?"

"Yes."

"When?"

"About three months ago. Before Easter, anyway."

"How close?"

"Very. We weren't sharing a flat or anything like that but we were . . . well, I suppose you'd call it old-fashioned courting. By that I mean my parents were involved, with Jimmy coming to the house a lot and having meals with us and discussing plans and things."

"Plans? The courting was with a view to marriage?"

"Yes."

"Were you engaged to be married?"

"Not exactly. Not officially, I suppose I mean. You see, Jimmy had set his heart on giving me a certain engagement ring. An expensive one. I told him it didn't matter about the ring, or any ring, if it came to that, but he insisted he was going to do things properly and he refused to get the ring until he had saved up a thousand pounds to pay for it on the spot. He used to joke about how he wasn't going to have his fiancée on the never-never." Her voice faltered a little and Masters could see incipient tears in her eyes. He paused just long enough for her to recover before continuing his questions.

"You used to sail with him?"

"I crewed for him. That's really how we began to get friendly. His old crew moved away and the man I used to sail with wanted to train his daughter, so I suppose I was a spare hand."

"He asked you to crew?"

"In just one race, one Sunday, when he was short-handed,

156

and one way or another it became a sort of permanent arrangement."

"Why didn't you bring the boat up together for the meeting?"

"It's not really up to the mark at the moment. We could have come, perhaps, if we'd had a new suit of sails, but they are quite expensive and Jimmy refused to buy them because, as I told you, he was saving up like mad."

"For a very good reason. The ring."

"Yes."

"So Jimmy accepted the offer to crew for Harry Martin?"

"That's right."

"Why didn't you come up here with him?"

"I'd have liked to, but I couldn't get the time off."

"Ah," said Masters. Both Pedder and Green sensed that this was the moment of truth. "Now, Janet, from what you have said so far, I gathered that if Jimmy had entered his Supra for the racing, you would have come up with him to crew. That means you could have got the time off at the time the entries had to be in. Yet when Jimmy decided to crew for Harry Martin, you couldn't get the time off. That suggests that the arrangement for Jimmy to crew for Harry Martin was a very late one. Am I right?"

She nodded. "Oh, yes. Harry's crew is a schoolmaster, and he knew right from the start he couldn't be at the Cullermouth Meeting. So Harry had arranged with somebody up here to crew for him."

"A member of the Cullermouth Club?"

"Yes."

"Who?"

"I don't know his name, except that though he wasn't a member of the Supra section up here he was a regular sailor in some other type of boat, and so crewing a Supra would be no different from what he was used to."

"I see. But presumably that arrangement fell through?"

"Only about a fortnight ago. Harry was in a bit of a fix then. He asked Jimmy if he would crew for him. Jimmy had some holiday to come from last year and he was in a position in his firm where he could take it virtually when he liked. When I said I couldn't make it at such short notice he was all set to refuse Harry's offer, but I knew he'd like a week up here near his parents and all round here where he was brought up, so I persuaded him to come. I was going to come up on Friday to stay the weekend with him at his parents' house and then travel back with him."

"Thank you," said Masters. "That is all very clear, and you have been most helpful."

"Have I? Really helpful, I mean?"

"You'll never know how much, love," said Green.

"Oh, good."

"By the way, Janet," said Masters, "what is your work?"

"I'm the personnel officer for the non-clerical female staff of Quartermains. Do you know the company?"

"I should do, my dear. You advertise widely enough."

She smiled at him. "Is that everything?"

"Yes, thank you."

"I promised to try and remember everything you asked me, you see. Mr Cleveland was very insistent. He'll want to know."

"I'm sure he will. Perhaps you will give him a message from Mr Green and myself?"

"Of course. What is it?"

"Just say that today is December the third and tomorrow will be the fifth."

She looked bewildered. "Will he understand that, because I certainly don't?"

"He'll explain it to you."

"Today is December the third and tomorrow will be the fifth?"

"Yes."

Pedder got to his feet. "Come on Janet. I'll take you back to the kitchen to say goodbye to the ladies while I have a final word with Mr Masters."

"I'll find my own way back, Mr Pedder. No need for you to come. You stay and have your talk."

When the door had closed behind her, Pedder turned to Masters. "Judder, you told that little lass that she had been a great help. All you did was have a cosy little chat. How could that help with this business up here?"

"It confirmed what I suspected. Jimmy Cleveland was a late replacement for Harry Martin's original crew member. So late, that not everybody knew about the switch. That in turn leads me to suppose that the man who dropped out was the intended victim. I can discover his name from Martin. With him in our sights I can line up my questions more accurately."

"From the message you've given that girl for Matt, I took it to mean you'll be finished tomorrow."

"I think so. All ready for you and yours to take over. Sandy Finch will manage very well from then on."

"In that case, I'll say goodnight. But ring me as soon as you've made an arrest. I shall want to know immediately, and so will Matt."

Masters nodded his agreement.

Green was up very early the next morning, ostensibly to wait for the milkman, but he had taken care to arm himself with the packet of Ovals. Nel, however, did not appear. As a consequence, he was a gloomy companion as Masters drove the Rover along the road to Wearbay. As they queued for a moment or two at the tunnel entrance to pay the toll, Berger and Tip came up behind them. The two cars travelled in convoy to the car park at Abbot's Haven.

"How did you two get on last night?" asked Masters as the four of them started to walk towards the clubhouse.

"It's difficult to say, Chief," replied Berger. "It was a nice party."

"Seemingly innocuous?"

"I'd have said so, but because we were keeping our eyes open we did see some things going on."

"As you'd expect," said Tip. "Mr Head and I played Peeping Toms on several . . . er . . . couplings, I think would be the best word, Chief."

"Involving the people we are interested in?"

"Oh, yes. It was in the line of duty, Chief. We weren't doing it for a cheap thrill."

"I didn't suggest you were, Tip."

They crossed the road before the ramp down into the little bay. Tip gestured to her right. "Those two huts over there were a favourite spot, Chief. One's the old wartime coastguard hut and the other belongs to the Sea Scouts. There are several boats and other bits and pieces around to provide cover."

"What for?" growled Green. "Watchers?"

"Watchers and watched," answered Tip quietly, surprised by the tone adopted by Green, who was usually most friendly towards her.

"What about you?" Masters asked Berger.

"I was taken for a . . . stroll . . . along the quay, Chief. After dark the seats along there were fairly popular."

"I can imagine."

"Mr Finch came. I think he found himself confined to the bar for the most part."

"Did anybody visit the camp site?"

"I didn't, Chief," said Berger. "I couldn't think of any excuse to get my partner down that way."

"I didn't go myself," said Tip, "but Mr Head used his meeting with the camping ladies yesterday morning as an excuse to follow somebody that way."

"Right. We'll hear all about it later."

Green plodded across the few feet of powdery sand to the steps leading on to the clubhouse verandah. "Breakfast," he grunted. "That's all I want to hear about right now."

"What's biting him, Chief?" asked Berger, falling back to join Masters.

"He's lost Nel."

"The dog?"

"Yes."

"But it isn't his to lose."

"No, but he values the friendship and he thinks she has deserted him."

160

"If anybody but you had told me that about him, Chief, I'd never have believed it."

"I'm a bit surprised myself."

"Chief!"

"Yes?"

"Now Tip's gone in with the DCI, I think I ought to tell you that she did a good job last night. She didn't like the assignment . . ."

"I realise that."

"And she had a bit of fighting off to do on her own account."

"Not from Mr Head, I hope:"

"No. He . . . and I . . . had to step in. He didn't do quite as much looking about him as he might have done because he was a bit worried about her. For the most part these people were very well behaved, but there were a few bravos who'd got too much booze on board, and Tip is a very attractive girl."

Masters smiled. "I've noticed you think so. We all do. I'm sorry if she was in any way . . ."

"She coped, Chief. She coped. But I don't know whether we uprooted any trees to speak of."

"Tell me later. Breakfast now."

Wednesday morning was a replica of that of Tuesday, except that today the Thames Estuary Trophy was to be competed for, with a second cup, the Bell Commemorative Rose Bowl, being raced for at the same time. The only difference between the two was that the latter would be presented to the first boat over five years old to cross the finishing line. A notice on the board announced that there was to be an Owners' Association Meeting in the clubhouse at six-thirty in the evening, preceding whatever jollification had been arranged for later.

The chatter was the same, the helpers were the same, the breakfast was the same and the weather was the same.

When Finch and Head joined them at the table, Masters said, "We can't discuss the events of last night at the moment.

However, I should like to know whether any of you saw anything which could be of use. Sandy?"

"I think so."

"Me, too," said Head.

"Thank you. Berger and Tip fancy they got a little, too. The important thing is that everybody involved should be strictly identified and then written up in the briefest possible way. I don't want any lurid details."

They all nodded their understanding of this order.

"Right. We'll get Stan to open the Dry Bar as soon as we've had breakfast and we'll confer up there. Then Ashley and I will be going out in the launch for an hour or two."

As a result of the conference upstairs, where Masters told them what he had learned from Janet Galliford the evening before and the deductions he considered had been confirmed by this, he allocated certain duties to each of them. By the time he had completed the briefing it was almost time for Ashley Head and himself to leave to pick up Harry Martin and to join the motor launch which had been laid on. This had come down the river, out of the mouth and then turned west to head into the little bay of Abbot's Haven. A hefty young policeman, in dark trousers and a white vest was at the wheel, just keeping enough way on his craft to enable him to stand off to the south of the main launch sites so as not to interfere with the dinghies taking to the water.

Green and Tip went about the first of their allotted tasks. They climbed up on to the bank of the dinghy park and approached the uniformed policeman keeping watch on Harry Martin's *Spearhead*. Green identified himself.

"Any attempts at interference, son?"

"No, sir. I took over at six. The PC I relieved said nothing had happened after he took over at midnight, though the chap on previous to him had to report a few goings on during the evening watch, sir."

"Anything definite in the way of an attempt to get at this boat?"

"He reckoned he thought there was, sir, but with all the

162

goings-on at the barbecue party he couldn't be absolutely sure."

"Right, lad. Have you had any breakfast?"

"At five o'clock, sir, before I came out."

"Okay. Do you know anything about boats? This sort, I mean?"

"A bit, sir. Most of us local lads do."

"Would you know what a mainsheet is?"

"The whole tackle, sir?"

"Just the rope, lad."

"Yes. I know what that is."

"Good. I want you to uncover this dinghy very, very carefully, touching nothing but the cover, and to tell me if the mainsheet is still there. Without touching it."

The young policeman took off his cap and put it with the uniform jacket which he had worn against the chill of the morning when first coming on duty, but which now hung over the low railing which divided the dinghy park from the moat. Then he went down on one knee and started to untie the knots of the lashing which passed under the keel to hold the cover in place.

Green turned to Tip. "Goldie's *Slowcoach* has gone from here," he said, "but it may not be launched yet. Go down to the water's edge and see. I'll watch from the top of the ramp. Give me a wave if he's still available. I don't want to stop him getting out to the start-line, but if this lad finds a mainsheet in this boat, I want Goldie to have a look. He said he'd be able to recognize the one he lost, so a quick shufti should settle the matter."

"How will I know if you want to see Goldie—if he's there?"

"Keep your eye on me, lass. I'll give you another wave if I want him."

Tip skittered down the ramp, her shoes sliding on the fine sand on the rubber tracks and her arms out shoulder high keeping her balance. Green lit a cigarette and stood watching her as she ran on to the soft sand and slowed to a fast walk. He had a guilty feeling that he had been a little too abrupt with her earlier on for no other reason than his own grumpiness at

Nel's desertion. He would have to heal the breach somehow, because he was fond of her. Then he found himself wondering whether he had ever felt guilty after the countless occasions on which he had been rude to male subordinates. He couldn't recall any such feelings and came to the reluctant decision that, good at the job though they may be, women detectives were a damn nuisance, no matter how charming.

At that moment the charming-damn-nuisance turned and waved and, after he had acknowledged, lifted her hand high again to point to a dinghy still on a trailer, waiting to get into the water.

Spearhead was about twenty yards away. Green had seen the young PC start carefully to fold back the cover down the port side of the dinghy, taking it back in a great fold the whole length of the hull and as far back as the hole in the centre line that accommodated the mast. Green wanted to shout to him to hurry, but in view of the orders about carefulness he had laid down, he restrained himself. Instead he strolled over and said reasonably enough, "Can you see a mainsheet, lad?"

"It's here, sir." The PC pointed to a coil of off-white rope, neatly tucked down alongside the centre-board housing.

"Thanks. Hold everything until I get back."

Goldie didn't like being brought back to the dinghy park by Tip. He said so to Green, who replied rather tartly that he and his colleagues were doing everything in their power to ensure the owner of *Slowcoach* would not miss his day's racing and if said owner would stop wasting time in complaining that objective might be more easily achieved.

"Now," said Green. "We've found a mainsheet in Mr Martin's boat. I want you to keep your hands in your pockets, but take a good look at the rope and tell me if it's yours."

"Is that all you brought me back for?"

"Take a look," commanded Green.

Goldie peered through his spectacles at the coiled mainsheet. "That's mine," he said, after the briefest of glances.

"You're sure?"

"Of course I'm sure."

"What makes you so certain?"

164

"The end of the damn thing. We don't whip these ropes, or at least I don't. Some people just burn them to seal them. I wrap a ribbon of plastic a couple of inches wide round mine and then shove it in a gas flame. The plastic melts and I have a seal two inches long instead of just an end that's been fused. And I use blue plastic for my seals as you'll see if you examine them very closely. And I do that because my wife buys blue plastic bags for use in her freezer. Now, if that's all, I'll be on my way, and I'll collect my property when I come ashore this afternoon."

"No, you won't lad. That's evidence. So just go and sail your boat. Oh, and good luck."

Goldie, without a word, hurried off to the launch site.

"Thanks, lad," said Green to the PC. "Would you mind putting it all back again now? After that we'll mind it for a bit while you go inside for a cup of coffee. But let me give you a warning. Before you do anything after leaving here, give your hands a good scrub. There's been cyanide around this tub."

"I see, sir. Not too good, that."

"It's killed one kid already. I don't want you to be the second one."

When the PC had disappeared down the steps into the clubhouse, Tip asked what finding the missing mainsheet meant.

"I can't say, lass, at least not at the moment, but I'll tell you one thing, and that is that I don't think his nibs has ever pulled a bigger boner than leaving this dinghy unguarded all yesterday."

"Be fair, sir," protested Tip. "It was the local scene-of-crime people who tied it down and said it could be left before ever the Chief was called in. They'd been over it and found nothing and said it was of no further significance. And one of the first things the Chief did yesterday morning was to assign Sergeant Berger to watch the dinghy park."

Green half sat on the low railing and took out his cigarette packet. "What you've said is right, love. For you, that is. But not for George Masters. He operates on a different plane. He

165

knows well enough that first the locals like Sandy Finch and Ashley Head shouldn't have made the mistake of taking the word of the SC for granted and that he shouldn't have compounded the felony by going along with it. That's why he got so insistent yesterday teatime that it should be closely guarded overnight."

"I still don't understand why."

"He'll accept the word of forensic and scene-of-crime boys that there's no cyanide in that boat, nor anything else of a toxic nature. But when they say everything is as it should be, they are going beyond their brief. For instance, at first glance that dinghy is just as it should be with all its bits and pieces there. Nothing missing, nothing extra. But are they the right bits and pieces? They don't know. A man like his nibs, me, and now you, should be sceptical. Little *Spearhead* here is a case in point. It should have a mainsheet and it has got a mainsheet. But it is not its own mainsheet. It belongs to the bloke next door who's just identified it."

"And the Chief expected that?"

"I think he did."

Tip joined him in leaning on the rail. "I see now," she said. "The Chief wants to know what happened to the original rope. The one he knows was nearly chafed through. That has some significance."

Green grinned at her. "You're half-way there, petal."

She stared for a moment and then the light dawned. "Two ropes, two problems," she said quietly. "The one in the wrong boat could perhaps be as significant as the one that's disappeared."

"Now you're thinking, lass. And that is the sort of thing that can always happen, so we—and that includes you—should never take anybody's word for these things until you've proved it for yourself."

"I won't—in future. And here's young Mr Plod, carrying his plastic cup of coffee. Or to be more accurate, should I say his plastic beaker of plastic coffee?"

"I think you should, love. And for that, you can have the privilege of buying me one. Only ask them for a bit of ceramic, will you. I like to get my mouth round a bit of pot and I like a handle to hold."

Finch and Berger were in the Dry Bar with the plan of the dinghy park the sergeant had drawn and annotated. The plan was laid out on one of the two writing tables that stood against the pillars of wall dividing the windows. To ensure privacy, Finch had called in another uniformed constable to stand by the door.

Four ashtrays kept the plan from rolling up. A box of fat-barrelled, felt-tipped text markers sat centre top. Finch had drawn up a chair on which was assembled a heap of papers, including his own lists and the brief reports of the barbecue watchers among others.

"Legend top left," said Finch. "What was it the Chief said? Blue for abroad, was it?"

"It doesn't matter," said Berger, "not if you're having a key."

"Right, Sergeant. Here's the list of the people identified from the photographs you took. Only eleven of them." Finch put the paper on the chart. "Put those in, while I sort out the job categories. After that it will be the travellers . . ."

"How do I get aboard?" asked Masters. "Paddle?"

"No, Chief. When you're ready I'll signal to the launch and he'll pull over to the first set of steps on the quay. He hasn't put in there yet because he doesn't want to get in the way of the Supras."

"I see. There are none of them over there."

"No, Chief, but there could be. You see there's a heavy rope looped from the mooring ring in the stonework close to the steps."

"Yes. It disappears in a loop into the water."

"And is tied to that stake inshore this side of the launch sites."

"Ah, yes. I've been wondering what that was for."

"In theory, if the weather makes it necessary, the dinghies can put a painter round that rope—it's just under the

167

surface, actually—and tie up there. They can lower their sails there if there's a blow while they're waiting, or alternatively they can haul themselves along it, in order, into the shore. In this weather it's not likely to be used, but it is one of the amenities laid on permanently here, and so everybody gives it a wide berth in case somebody might want to use it."

"I see. We'll go along to the steps, shall we?"

Head turned and put two fingers into his mouth. The resultant high-pitched whistle caused the PC in the launch to look their way. Head waved an arm and, receiving an acknowledgement, turned to accompany Masters and Harry Martin to the quay.

Masters had very little experience of boats. He had, on occasions, needed to take a trip on a river police launch, but that was about the extent of his wet-bobbing since rowing in a four when at school. But he enjoyed this. Standing in the cockpit beside the helmsman who used a high chair on the port side aft of the cabin, he had a good view over the bow and, indeed, all around him. The sun, already strong, glistened on the almost smooth water which gradually changed in colour from brown-grey to a deeper green. Ahead of them, some of them more than a mile away, were dotted the multi-coloured sails of scores of craft. Light, stillness, peace, except for the throb of their own engine and the disturbed area of their wake.

"What speed are you doing?"

"About seven knots, sir. I could get another one or two out of her, if you like."

"No, thank you. The race has not started yet."

"No, sir. I can't see what signal the start boat has got up. There's not enough wind to . . . ah! They're using a gun, sir."

"Gun?" Masters had been a little taken aback by the sound of the distant boom over the water.

"They call it a gun, sir. Some people actually use them."

"I've seen those cannon lined up outside the yacht club at Cowes."

"That's the sort of thing, sir. But this is a firework sort of thing. A pyrotechnic bombard."

"I see."

"So there's five minutes to go before the off, Chief."

"Thank you, Ashley. I'd like us to take up station—if that's the correct word—close to the buoy where the craft have to turn from a run to a beat." He turned to Harry Martin who was sitting quietly on the cushions in the stern. "Have I got that right, Mr Martin? Was it at that point that you handed over to Jimmy Cleveland?"

"Yes. As we were coming up to the buoy. Perhaps thirty or forty yards before we were due to round. We could manage to change over fairly easily because we had quite a lot of clear water around us and the manoeuvre was not going to result in us fouling anybody else."

"Thank you."

"In that case," said the launch helmsman, "I'd better stand off the buoy upwind. I'll have to keep well away, sir, because some of them will want to take it wider than others, but with your binoculars you'll be able to see the manoeuvring quite clearly."

"I leave it to you. But I'm not interested in the boats and sails themselves. I want to see the antics of the people on board."

"Well, sir, there's no saying when the movement of a boat won't bring a sail across to hide the crew, and I'll have to keep a bit of way on the launch, so I'll patrol up and down a line about thirty yards from the buoy. That will be parallel to the course the dinghies will be sailing, of course."

"Can't we get closer than thirty yards?"

Harry Martin said, "Any closer, Mr Masters, and you'll be interfering with the race. You should be able to see well enough from thirty yards."

"Very well. I'll have a pair of the binoculars, please, Sandy."

Harry Martin got to his feet and joined Masters. "I think you're in luck's way, Chief Superintendent."

"Oh, how's that?"

"Because I think there'll be a beat on the third leg of the

first round today. From number three marker to number one."

"That's on the triangular round."

"That's right. You'll get the same beat on the second, oblong round, of course, but that could very well mean waiting for a couple of hours. As it is they'll have the wind on the starboard beam for the first leg and the port beam for the second, so they won't take much more than a quarter of an hour or twenty minutes each for the leading boats."

"So we want to be to the east of marker three in about half an hour or so, is that it?"

"That's right. The rounding marks are those large, vertical, cylindrical buoys. Positions are deceptive out here, but number one is the windward mark and the start line seems to be level with it to the east. Ah! That's it. They're away."

The boom echoed over the water a second time.

"No recall, either," said Martin. "That's lucky, but one or two have been caught with their pants down. See! Two of them facing directly away, and several tacking about to get on course."

Masters watched through the binoculars. The PC helmsman, with plenty of time in which to take up his position near marker three, reduced speed to make it easier to use binoculars. The launch tittupped forward, just nodding to the slight sea and the gently increased wind out here away from the coast.

By the time the launch was in position, just one or two of the dinghies had forged ahead from the main body of the fleet which had not yet shaken itself out, as it would later, to cover all the legs of the course. The PC helmsman throttled back, leaving himself just enough power to patrol the line he had suggested. The line actually became a very elongated narrow figure of eight as the need to turn through 180 degrees at each end dictated some such manoeuvre. The cross piece of the eight was the nearest point to the marker. Masters pronounced himself satisfied with the arrangement and sent

170

Ashley Head, armed with binoculars, to stand in the bow pulpit.

"What am I looking for, Chief?" asked Head quietly.

"If you see what I hope you'll see, you'll know what it is. I won't tell you, because I want a truly independent witness."

Head shrugged and moved off down the narrow catwalk alongside the cabin to reach his appointed position.

After another ten minutes the first boat started to round the marker. Masters watched them closely, but saw nothing of what he wanted to see.

After a good many craft had rounded the mark, Masters said to Martin, "What was it they were approaching on?"

"From mark two to three?"

"Yes."

"A reach. The wind comes over the side of the boat, so the sail is about half out, as you can see."

"And when you handed over to Jimmy Cleveland the other morning?"

"Oh, you want to see that? We were on the oblong course. So we were running before the wind down to the buoy, and once we had rounded it—a hundred and eighty degree turn—we were beating into it. It was dead against us."

"Thank you. How soon will we see that?"

"All those that have rounded mark three are already beating up to mark one. You can see them tacking about with their sails close-hauled. Once they've rounded mark one they won't dog-leg out to mark two, they'll run back here again to mark three and then have to beat back a second time to mark one for the start of round three."

"I think I've got that. How long will there be to wait?"

"I should think another half hour at least for the leading boats. They'll do the running leg much quicker than the beat leg, of course."

Masters started to pack his pipe with Warlock Flake. The helmsman, seeing that observation was over for the time being, said, "Mr Head told me to bring a gallon thermos of coffee from the canteen, sir. And I brought a packet of coconut biscuits if you'd like . . ."

171

"I could do with a mug of coffee, please."

"I'll take the wheel," offered Head, coming back to the cockpit. He turned to Masters. "Sorry, Chief, but I saw nothing out of the ordinary."

"No more did I, Ashley. Better luck next time."

And, indeed, it was better luck. The first boat to round mark three, at least forty yards ahead of its nearest rival, gave Masters what he wanted to see. An excited shout from Head up in the pulpit showed he had noted it, too. As far as Masters could tell, knowing none of the finer points of sailing, the dinghy was approaching the mark at a run, with the sail right out at 90 degrees to the hull. The helmsman, therefore, had his mainsheet fully extended. All thirty feet of it, running from his own hands through two pulleys in the centre block of the boat to two on the boom and then back again to the centre. Five lengths to and from the boom which was hard up against the wire shroud which held the mast up on that side. By watching carefully, Masters could see that the helm had jammed the mainsheet into a cleat while running, to take the strain off his hands and arms. But as he came to turn the rounding mark, taking him from the run to the beat, there was the sudden flurry of activity needed to turn the boat through 180 degrees to get on to the return course with no loss of time or space. Because the sail had to come into the boat for the boom to lie along its length, the helmsman was suddenly faced with the task of hauling in thirty feet of rope and coping with it on something like a four or five to one purchase. Masters watched, fascinated, and let out an audible sigh of relief. The helmsman pulled in an armslength of rope with the hand not occupied with the tiller, but instead of wasting the time necessary to jam the rope he had won into a cleat before pulling in other armslength, he put it in his mouth. His teeth held it firm while another yard came in, and then the mouth grip was changed to that spot on the rope. The skilled helm, showing he knew the tricks of the trade! The tricks that were saving precious seconds to take him to the front of the fleet and keep him there.

Masters kept his glasses riveted on the man's face. By the time his craft was fully on the beat, having lost not a second or a yard in rounding the mark, a small red mark had appeared at the corner of his mouth. Masters could actually see the tip of the tongue come out to lick away the tiny drop of blood.

Oblivious of the passage of time, Masters stayed watching closely until most of the fleet had rounded the buoy. He managed to get a clear view of eight of the helms who used their mouths when hauling their sails hard in at the mark. Satisfied, he lowered his binoculars.

"Did Jimmy Cleveland use his mouth when changing from the run to the beat?" he asked Martin.

The sailor, grey-faced, nodded his head.

"Do you?"

"No. I tried it once, but never again."

"But you know what there was on the rope that Jimmy used?"

"I can only assume it was impregnated with cyanide."

"Right."

"So that's how . . . how he got it."

"In view of the fact that you say he neither ate nor drank anything that morning, I think we must assume we have now discovered the means by which it was fed to him."

Masters called Head back from the pulpit and asked the helmsman of the launch to return to Abbot's Haven.

"You saw them, Chief?"

"Eight, or so."

"I saw eight, too. But how could you guess? I mean . . . well, you say you know nothing about sailing."

"The cyanide had to be on or in something in the dinghy, and that something had to go into Jimmy Cleveland's mouth. I scrutinized everything on one of these craft, and the only thing I could discover that might conceivably go in was a rope. And even that idea only came to me after I saw a dog retrieve a stick from the sea. The way the stick stuck across the corners of the dog's mouth made me recall that I had seen some of these sailors with small lesions at the mouth corners."

173

"So you took photographs and then came out here to prove it for yourself?"

"That's about the size of it."

Harry Martin had been listening. "It is only possible to use your mouth for holding a rope in weather like this, when the wind is not too strong. At least for this particular manoeuvre."

"Why?" asked Head. "Because a sudden gust could pull your teeth out?"

"That's right."

"Particularly if you have pot ones?"

Martin smiled wanly. "I've seen some bleeding lips after races. That's one of the reasons why I don't use the trick myself. And I'm bloody pleased I don't, otherwise . . ."

"Quite," said Masters. "You might have suffered the fate of Jimmy Cleveland."

"Don't get me wrong, Mr Masters. I'd have done anything to prevent it happening to Jimmy."

"I'm sure you would, Mr Martin. Now, before you leave us, I'd like you to give Inspector Head a written statement that Jimmy used his mouth on the mainsheet when rounding the mark from a run to a beat, and then hold yourself in readiness in case there is something more I need to ask you."

"Right. Can I join my wife?"

"I'd rather you didn't or, rather, if you give me your solemn promise not to mention to her or to anybody else what we have discovered this morning, then you may join her for lunch—after finishing with us."

"Thank you. I'll keep your secret."

"Mrs Martin will question you, you know."

"Inevitably. I shall just say you felt you needed to watch a race at close quarters and took me along as guide."

"Excellent. I shall see you later, Mr Martin."

"You were right, then?" asked Green as Masters joined him in the dinghy park.

"Yes. He mouthed the rope. How have you got on?"

"It's there. The next door neighbour's missing mainsheet.

Or rather it was there. I got Goldie to identify it by his particular way of sealing the ends, then I had a scene-of-crime merchant come down and collect it for testing."

"What did he say to that?"

"Admitted nobody had tested it for cyanide. He said there was no point in doing so because the rope is terylene and won't soak up liquids, and in any case the cyanide salts are so soluble in water that the rope only had to go over the side for anything on it to be washed away."

"To which, no doubt, you made a suitable reply?"

Tip, who was standing nearby, giggled.

"What's up with you, love?"

"The memory of what you said to the SC man."

"Forthright, was it?" asked Masters.

"Very. Boiled down, the DCI told him that if he was so sure it was free of cyanide would he kindly lick a few feet of it. 'Stick it in your cake-hole and make a meal of it' were the words used at that point. Some of the others are not repeatable, Chief. But the DCI did point out that though terylene would not soak up fluids, the rope was made of hundreds of strands between which it was just possible some minute trace of cyanide might still be detectable. The SC man, in view of the fact that he had refused to put the rope near his mouth or to handle it without rubber gloves on, could hardly deny his suggestion, so off he went with it in a plastic bag, and somebody in some lab is, I expect, now carefully unravelling it ready for testing."

"Excellent. Now, how about a drink after our successful morning?"

"Not a bad idea. We can go up to the Dry Bar for it. Sandy allowed Stan, the steward, to open it for business about half an hour ago."

"Good. But I shall still want this dinghy under observation. Tip, make sure that's done, will you, please?"

"Observation, Chief? Not guard?"

"Clandestine observation, Tip. Our man can find a bit of shade from which to keep an eye on it."

"Why not have it towed to the station, Chief?"

Green looked at her in despair.

"Have I said something outrageous?"

"You have, petal. As long as it stays here there is always the slight chance that somebody—and I don't mean Goldie—might wander this way in the hope of retrieving that rope. Not while a dirty great PC is sitting on its centre-board, of course, but once he has ostensibly been withdrawn, then our desperado might chance his arm."

"I see. But he had all Monday night and most of Tuesday when he could have done that and he didn't."

"More fool he, love. But his nibs is not saying he will come. Just that he might."

Tip, still looking sceptical, went off to arrange the observation.

"Where's Mr Finch?"

Berger was alone in the Dry Bar.

"He went off to check on one or two points in his list, Chief."

"I see. Would you please go downstairs and find Mr Head? He'll be in one of the offices taking a statement from Harry Martin. Tell him I want him to get hold of Martin's old mainsheet—the one that was nearly worn through—and keep it handy."

"I know, Chief. The one Jimmy Cleveland complained about."

"That's it. Martin must know where it is."

Berger nodded towards the table where the box of felt markers, the now-rolled-up chart and a file of reports were neatly stacked. "Will you look after that lot for me until I get back?"

"Leave it all with us."

"Cold lager, George?"

"I think so, Bill. But it's on me."

"Not that I mind you paying, but tell me, why the sudden generosity?"

"Just to acknowledge the help you've given, Bill. Your interest in Nel and playing with the little brown dog down on

176

the beach gave me the idea about the rope."

"What about Wanda? She was the one who noticed that some of the sailors had sore mouths."

"I'm not forgetting that, Bill. Is there a barman about?"

"Shop," called Green loudly.

There was no reply, but a moment later Sam, carrying a book, came in from the sun-deck outside the bar. "Sorry, gentlemen, but your colleague asked me if I minded waiting outside."

"Not to worry, son," grunted Green. "We're being a bit of a nuisance to you, I suppose . . ."

"Hardly! I'd rather sit out there and read than sit on a bar stool."

"In that case," said Masters, "have one with us. Can you drink lager?"

"Try me."

"In that case, three lagers, please."

"You'd better add three more long something-or-others to that order, George. Wanda and my missus are just arriving with the boy."

Masters glanced at his watch. "Lunchtime already? There's a hell of a lot I want to do, Bill."

"Have lunch," counselled Green, "then tell us all what you want and we'll co-operate in getting down to it."

Masters grinned. "It's just that I told that girlie to tell Matt Cleveland we'd finish today and there's our own holiday to think about. After all the trouble Doris took to arrange it I don't want to spoil it completely."

"You won't, chum. Ah, here they are. Drinks coming up."

"We've had a lovely morning," said Wanda. "Some of the mothers had taken a party of tiny ones on to the beach in Wearbay and Michael was able to join them. He thoroughly enjoyed himself."

"Good." Masters kissed her soundly on the forehead. "How are you getting on?"

"Famously. I've solved the mystery of the mouth lesions and how Jimmy Cleveland was caused to ingest the cyanide— if you don't mind that way of putting it."

"I understand."

Berger returned. "Shall I go down and fetch the grub up, Chief?"

"If you please."

"There are fifty or sixty little horrors down there and three mums armed with wooden spoons keeping them quiet. Wonderful how quiet a tap with the rounded bowl of a spoon will keep a child." Berger left. Wanda laughed.

It was obvious to everybody that Masters hurried the lunch break and was anxious to get back to business as soon as possible. Sensing this, Wanda got to her feet as soon as the alfresco meal was over. "Doris and I want to do some shopping, darling. Probably in Durham. Michael can have a sleep in the car. The movement will send him off."

"Right, poppet. We'll be home as soon as we can, and that means, at a guess, about eight o'clock. And while you're out shopping, would you get in enough food for the two sergeants as well? I'd like them to join us for supper."

"Nothing easier," said Wanda, picking up her son. "We shall look forward to seeing them."

Masters got down to business immediately.

"I'd like to see the original mainsheet, Ashley. Fetch it now, please."

Head went off.

"Sandy, I see you say Goatcher is a civil servant."

"Yes, Chief."

"Yet according to your notes he went on a business trip to Zambia."

"Yes, Chief."

"Normal civil servants don't go on business trips. They sit at home and drink tea. Please go to your office and phone London to find out which department he is in and so forth. Everything about him, please, as quickly as possible."

Finch went off.

Masters turned to Berger. "Have you identified the man who left the caravan yesterday afternoon?"

"Yes, Chief. It was Hunt."

178

"He's on your chart, and the woman involved?"

"Both in green, Chief."

"The husband?"

"He's not marked in."

"My mistake. I should have included aggrieved parties. Colour him in, too."

"Green, Chief?"

"Yes, please."

"Tip."

"Yes, Chief?"

"I want to see Vera Bartram as soon as she's ashore. Take over a committee room of some sort for the interview."

"Right, Chief."

"Bill."

"What can I do?"

"Stay with me, for everything."

"Anything you say."

Head came back with *Spearhead*'s original mainsheet and handed it to Masters.

"This has been cut, Ashley."

"In two places, Chief, and not where it was worn, either."

"Bill?"

"Razor blade," replied Green. "A quick slash, if you'll forgive the phrase."

"Bag it, please, Ashley."

Head went off.

"Berger."

"Yes, Chief?"

"What does it look like now?"

"Inconclusive at the moment, Chief."

Masters rose to look at the chart. "You haven't got Hunt in coloured yellow."

"Sorry, Chief, but he isn't a crew member."

"He was to have been. Put him in and then go and find Martin. Ask him whether Hunt used his mouth on ropes."

"Yes, Chief."

Tip returned. "The room is ready when you want it, Chief."

"Thank you, Tip."

"Hang on a moment," expostulated Green. "You're doing it all in shorthand. When are we going to know something?"

"I'll explain. But first, Tip, please tell Mr Head I shall want to see Hunt as soon as possible. He's to find him and bring him here if need be. Even if he's at his shop. You can help him."

"Right, Chief. In the interview room?"

"Please, Tip."

After the WDS had gone, Green said: "All right, George, spill it."

Masters spoke for some minutes.

"So it all depends on what Sandy turns up."

"Yes."

Berger returned. "Martin says Hunt used his mouth on the rope, Chief."

"Thank you. Colour him appropriately on the chart, please."

Green said, "So he was to have been the victim?"

"I'm certain of it."

"Fine. We know the victim, the means and the method, and it all points to one man, so far. What if . . . ?"

The telephone behind the bar rang. The student barman, Sam, answered it and then called over, "It's for you, Mr Masters. Sandy Finch."

"Department of Trade and Industry, Chief. Minerals and Metals Division. It's in Whitaker. But I rang London. He's in the Copper Branch."

"And his trip to Zambia?"

"Was to the copper belt towns."

"Thank you for ringing, Sandy. Write out a report and then get back here."

Masters returned to Green. "The same man. Went to the copper fields in Zambia."

Green whistled. "Easy to get hold of the stuff in the plants there."

"I'm certain of it."

"So now you've got everything except motive."

180

"We've got that, too. It was his caravan I saw Hunt leave. It was his missus who kissed Hunt. It was his missus Ashley followed back to the camp site last night and saw her joining Hunt."

"Still a bit thin though, isn't it?"

"We'll thicken it up."

"Right. Means, motive, method, opportunity, but very little material evidence except that slashed rope."

"And an impregnated one, besides a dead body."

"You'll need more."

"I want to impound *Slowcoach* as soon as it comes ashore. If I'm right and he impregnated the rope inside it, there could still be traces of cyanide on the woodwork or in the bilges."

"Are there any quick tests?"

"I think the Prussian Blue one is the quickest. But there are a number of suitable chemical tests—silver nitrate, Liebig's, Schilt, benzidine-copper. I suppose the quickest will take an hour or two."

The phone again.

"Sandy here, Chief. Forensic have found traces of cyanide in and on the rope."

"Thank you. Would you tell them to stand by for about three o'clock. We shall be sending them a dinghy. I want the whole of the inside of the hull testing."

"*Spearhead*?"

"No. *Slowcoach*."

"You're moving, Chief."

"I want to get back to my holiday. I'll see you as soon as you can get back here. As quickly as possible please."

"Right, Chief."

"Cyanide in the rope?" asked Green.

Masters nodded.

"Now what?"

"I want Sandy to pick him up as soon as they land, and you to pick up *Slowcoach*. Berger will help you."

"In that case," said Green, "I'll go and arrange the tow. I'll borrow Martin's road trailer."

"Try to borrow his car, too. It will have a tow bar."

"Right. So long."

"Sandy will tell you where to take it or give you a guide."

Green waved and left the Dry Bar. Berger came over to Masters. "The chart looks conclusive enough now, Chief."

"Thank you. But I've got to have statements to support it."

Tip returned. "Mr Head has got Hunt in the office, Chief. He was sitting on the verandah with two or three women."

"Including Mrs Goatcher?"

Tip nodded.

"I shall want to see her, too. After Hunt."

"Do you want me to tell her?"

"No. Stay here and mind the shop. Perhaps you can watch her movements from here."

"Sergeant Berger? What's he going to do?"

"Report to the DCI." He turned to Berger. "Help him take up *Slowcoach*. He's trying to get Martin's road trailer at the moment. Go and help him."

"Yes, Chief."

"I don't know how long I'll be, Tip."

Hunt made no secret of it. He had known Avril Goatcher for over a year. He asserted that no matter what other woman he may have played around with from time to time, she was the one for him and she reciprocated. She had even bought the van herself so that they had a mobile meeting place at open weekends. No, he hadn't known anybody else had known. Yes he had pulled out as Martin's crew because Mrs Goatcher had learned she could definitely get up to Cullermouth. He was more than shocked, he was scared stiff at the idea of being an intended murder victim. Yes, he would make and sign a full and detailed statement. Yes, he was sure Avril Goatcher would do the same.

Avril Goatcher came up to Hunt's expectations. They would report at the Wearbay police station forthwith to make the statements. Masters sent Tip with them to make sure what was recorded was what was needed.

*

Sandy Finch and Ashley Head waited for Goatcher. Green and Berger waited for *Slowcoach*. Masters waited for Vera Bartram. He wasn't too worried, now he had statements from Hunt and Mrs Goatcher, but he felt more evidence would be reassuring.

Vera Bartram was not going to tell tales.

Not even to help solve a murder? The biggest crime in the calendar? Far greater than moral turpitude.

Put like that . . .

All Masters wanted to know was whether there had been a clandestine affair between Mrs Goatcher and Mr Hunt.

Yes.

Details? Not lurid, of course.

Vera Bartram had become aware of it only because she had seen Goatcher, at a race meeting last autumn, hidden in some bushes and watching his own caravan. Vera Bartram had herself kept watch, unbeknown to Goatcher, and seen Hunt leave the van some time later. She had made it her business to warn Mrs Goatcher who had not been disposed to listen. Once she had become aware of the affair, Vera Bartram had found it difficult not to notice all manner of signs that the affair was still continuing.

Masters thanked her, apologised for holding her up, and let her go.

Green joined him in the Dry bar.

"The boat's gone, George. Berger and a local PC have taken it. Sandy and Ashley have taken Goatcher."

"Thank you, Bill."

"Where's Tip?"

"Thanking the powers-that-be for the use of their office."

"I could murder a cup of tea, George."

"I've no doubt you can get one downstairs."

"Shall I bring you one?"

"Yes, please. I'm going to ring Pedder. He asked me to let him know . . ."

Green came back with the tea.

"What did Alf say?"

"He's coming straight over. He'll be at the Wearbay nick at

half-past-four for a full run down."

"An hour from now. He's not wasting much time."

"I asked him to make it as soon as possible."

"Why."

"Because I'm supposed to be on holiday and I want to get back to it. Oh, by the way thanks for the tea."

"Think nothing of it. I'll let everybody know about the meeting with Alf, shall I?"

"Yes, please."

Masters looked around him, and then turned his attention to the plan Berger had drawn up and annotated with Finch's help. He studied it carefully for a minute or two before starting to speak.

"As I think you all know, Jimmy Cleveland was not the first choice of crew for *Spearhead*. His girlfriend, Janet, told us that he was a late replacement for a local man who, though not a member of the Supra Association and so not accustomed to racing in such boats, was nevertheless a dinghy owner and a capable helm in another class. Most helms are proficient at crewing, and I believe Harry Martin liked having a crew who could helm. Certainly the schoolmaster who regularly crewed for him was a skilled helm, and so was Jimmy Cleveland—a fact which probably influenced Martin's choice when he had to find a last-minute replacement.

"It is likely then, that few people, except those in his own immediate club down south, knew that Jimmy would be replacing the crew whose name appeared in the original printed lists for this meeting. That led us to suppose that the intention to commit murder up here concerned not Jimmy Cleveland, but the original crew."

"From what you've just said," interrupted Pedder, "it also means that the murderer is unlikely to have been a member of Jimmy's own club, otherwise he'd have known of the switch."

"Quite right, sir. That is a point which would have been mentioned later. It helped a lot in narrowing the field. Or so we hoped."

184

"You mean it didn't?"

"Many of the steps we have taken to exclude or even include people have obviously been little or no direct use, sir, but we had to take them, nonetheless. We simply had to cast around. There were no clues for us except the identity of the poison. We simply had to start a blanket operation. One of those blankets with holes in them, admittedly."

"Air-o-cell, they're called," said Tip.

"I'll keep my trap shut," said Pedder.

"Please don't, sir. Everybody here is entitled to ask questions. Indeed, is expected to."

"Fair enough, Judder."

"Thank you, sir. I'm going to skip now to the method used to administer the poison. First of all, however, I should tell you that there are quite a number of different cyanide preparations, liquids, gases and solids. I think we can ignore anything but the solids—in fact, forensic have informed me that they suspected sodium cyanide in the body and now have discovered traces of it in the mainsheet used in the boat Jimmy Cleveland was crewing on Monday. But the thing to remember is that most of the cyanide solids are listed as soluble in water or very soluble in water. Sodium cyanide is very soluble. Please consider for a moment what that means. It means that with very little water added to the salt one can get a highly concentrated solution.

"I have mentioned the mainsheet. That is a thirty-foot rope constantly in use for controlling the boat. Something we none of us here knew was that, very often, especially in light winds and when rounding a mark from a run to a beat, a good helmsman will save time by hauling in that rope, an arm's length at a time, and holding it in his mouth to prevent it running out again. The accepted alternative is to jam the rope in a cleat after each pull-in, but this takes more time than using the mouth, for obvious reasons."

"I'm coming in again," said Pedder. "Once you learned that fact you knew for sure the murderer was a sailor."

"We certainly assumed that, sir. It was a nice confirmation to have. Now, to get back to strong solutions of cyanide and

185

ropes that go in mouths. I don't have to explain that, by doctoring the other with the one, a pretty certain method of administering a lethal dose to anybody who mouths ropes is achieved. I know that modern ropes don't actually soak in water as, for instance cotton rope would. But soaked in a strong solution, with the fibres and strands probably eased apart to take the mixture into the body of the rope, the absorbency matters not at all. I said sodium cyanide needs very little water to make a strong solution. It would, therefore, dry fairly quickly, leaving the poison dabbed about on the surface and clinging to inner fibres. There was one possible snag from the murderer's point of view. Had the mainsheet gone overboard and been dragged in the water for even a very short time, the rope would probably have been cleansed and non-poisonous by the time Jimmy Cleveland put it to his mouth. Sad to say, good sailors make a point of not allowing their various ropes to trail in the water, and both Jimmy and Harry Martin were good sailors."

"Still," said Pedder, "if the murderer could have got his hand on the rope later, all he would have had to do is dunk it in a bucket of water to get rid of all the evidence."

"Just so, sir."

Finch groaned aloud. "And we withdrew the guard from that boat because forensic said they'd finished with it and there was nothing there for us."

"You what?" demanded Pedder, scowling across at Finch.

Masters stepped in quickly.

"The fault was mine, sir. Sandy had a guard on until after I arrived yesterday morning, but I gave no instructions that it was to continue. Fortunately, I had Sergeant Berger round there, and we restationed the guard later."

"Thank heaven for that."

"So we know how the cyanide was administered, and we know it wasn't intended for young Jimmy because he wasn't supposed to be in the boat. Neither was it for Martin, because he doesn't mouth his mainsheet. So who was it intended for? Clearly somebody—either helm or crew—who did use his mouth to hold the rope. In the hope of identifying the real victim, or at least hoping to limit the numbers among whom he could be found, we yesterday took photographs of everybody who showed the slightest sign of a lesion round the mouth. Although I laid this on personally, I was not too sanguine about finding the intended victim among them."

"Why not?" demanded Pedder.

"Because, sir, I reckoned I knew the poison was meant for whoever was to crew Martin's boat and none of those in the photographs was likely to have been he."

"Good point."

"But if I was right about that, then whoever our murderer was must have been sufficiently aware of Harry Martin's predilections to know, first, that Martin never put the mainsheet in his mouth and, second, that he was in the habit of handing the tiller over to his crew whenever they were approaching a beat. In this connection it is worth remembering that Martin always liked a good helm to crew for him, a fact which also must have been known to our man." Masters looked across at Pedder. "And those points, sir, argued that the murderer must have been very knowledgeable indeed about Martin's habits, which suggested that, despite what was said earlier, he must have been a member of the same club."

"I jumped into that one with both feet, didn't I, Judder?"

"I'm afraid you did, sir, but you're not the only one of us to have made a bosh shot."

"Nice of you to say so. But how did you resolve the point about the murderer not knowing about the change in *Spearhead*'s crew even though he was a member of the same section in the same club?"

Masters smiled. "We should ask Sandy the answer to that, sir. He's been cursing me up hill and down dale because I asked him to find out which of these people had been abroad and where and when. Unfortunately, my instructions couldn't be too precise as to times and areas and so on, so the task was a big one."

"You mean the bastard was away on holiday for some time until just before he came up here?"

"Not on holiday, sir. Abroad on business."

"Same thing."

"Not quite, sir, as Sandy will tell you. I had him asking about holidays. I should have stipulated being abroad for any reason whatsoever."

"I see. He missed this one, did he?"

"Shall we say it was a late discovery, sir. But Sandy's inquiries were directed at other things as well. I thought perhaps cyanide would be more easy to get in certain places abroad than in this country."

"I'm damn sure it is."

"Quite, sir. So, where are we now? We have the method of administering the poison. We wanted to know who it was for. I must admit it took me some time to realize that Jimmy was probably only a stand-in crew, that is why I needed to speak to Janet last night, sir. Once she had confirmed my thinking, all I had to do was to ask Harry Martin for the name of Jimmy's predecessor."

"Who was it, Chief?" asked Head.

Green snorted. "Mr Big, lad."

"Maurice Hunt?"

"The same."

There was some movement among the people listening to Masters.

"But, Chief . . ."

"Yes, Tip?"

She glanced across at Green.

"Go on," grunted Green. "Say it. I told you that he was running after little Mrs Nancy Claybourn, so, who from a club in the south of England would want to nobble him? Alec Claybourn might, of course, but unlikely. He sailed a little Mirror dinghy. Not in the same class as the Supras, so he wouldn't get to know anything about the way Harry Martin handled a boat."

"I added to that," said Head. "What I picked up definitely linked Hunt with Nancy Claybourn."

"But not exclusively, Ashley. This was another place where we could have slipped up. You reported that Hunt is a known womanizer. What we should have realized is that the Nancy

188

Claybourn affair may have only been a temporary one or, rather, a fill-in when a bigger affair was intermittently interrupted."

"I don't pretend to know what that means," protested Pedder.

"It means, sir, that Hunt was so much of a womanizer that though he much preferred one other particular woman to his wife, he was prepared, when his light o'love was not available, to find a substitute for her. In other words, he wanted a woman on his doorstep, no matter how great his feeling for the one down south whom he really wanted."

"A fill-in, you said?"

Masters nodded.

"For a woman from the south?"

"Yes."

"Who?"

"Avril Goatcher."

A little gasp went up. "You shouldn't have been surprised. You, Ashley, told me I had described Maurice Hunt to a T when I asked you to find out who he was. You all heard that. And I mentioned Avril Goatcher by name and Hunt as a visitor to her van. And if you had read the reports you would all see that Mr Head visited the camp site last night and saw the two in circumstances which he delicately describes as 'close'."

"But Goatcher, Chief! The mainsheet that killed Jimmy Cleveland came from his boat."

"That's right."

"But he didn't give it to Jimmy, because I heard Goldie say Goatcher had not been near the club on Monday. He said he'd gone sight-seeing."

"That's precisely what he did, or so I imagine. I think he followed his wife to Hunt's house or wherever they went together. We have learned Mrs Hunt was in Leeds, shopping, on Monday, so the coast was clear."

"It's still a bit of a mystery, Chief."

"I'm sorry. Everybody knows that Martin's mainsheet was badly worn on Saturday according to Jimmy Cleveland. But they had to use it on Sunday because the chandler's van doesn't do its rounds on Saturday evenings."

"The driver goes to the pictures," said Green.

"Something of that sort. But he did fetch up after the racing on Sunday afternoon. Harry Martin ordered a new mainsheet. The correct rope for it was not on the van. The driver promised to bring it on Monday afternoon. Is everybody clear about that?"

"Got it, Chief."

"On Monday morning, Harry Martin forgot his tool box. While he went back to the hotel to pick it up, Jimmy Cleveland rigged *Spearhead*. He found the mainsheet had, by now been cut through and totally useless. But he remembered that Goldie wasn't sailing *Slowcoach* in that day's race. So Jimmy borrowed Goldie's mainsheet. He pulled it through the tackle on the boom and then reeved it through *Spearhead*'s boom block. The intention was to put it back in *Slowcoach* on Monday afternoon so that it would be there for Goldie on Tuesday morning. Meanwhile the chandler would have brought a new rope for *Spearhead*. Has everybody understood that bit?"

"Sticking with that rope," continued Masters after everybody had signified they had understood him, "I would like to remind you that on Tuesday morning Goldie was complaining that his mainsheet had disappeared. He had to send Goatcher off somewhere to buy or borrow another one. At that time I had no idea of the significance of the mainsheet, nor did I know it was nestling beside the dagger-board casing in *Spearhead*. Fortunately for us, at that time *Spearhead* was still under guard, otherwise Goatcher might have found Goldie's mainsheet, accidentally-on-purpose, in *Spearhead* and cleansed it by putting it over the side once *Slowcoach* had been launched."

"But the poisoned mainsheet was still there this morning?" asked Pedder.

"Yes, sir."

"But surely . . . no, I don't get it, Judder. Are you saying Goatcher poisoned that rope?"

"Yes, sir."

"And left it in the boat he was crewing in?"

"Yes, sir."

"When?"

"I believe fairly early on Sunday evening. It was very easy to do, sir. The rope is attached to the tackle on the boom which lies along the top of the hull. Probably it was coiled up on the floorboards or a thwart, very easy to get at. If that was the case, Goatcher wouldn't even have to move it. I imagine the solution was in some sort of squeeze bottle—perhaps an empty washing-up-liquid container. With the rope coiled in a circle all he had to do was raise the boat cover on that side and spray the stuff all over the coil. I said he probably parted some strands. It seems as though he did, but even so it would be a short job. And if anybody who mattered saw him there, what the hell? He was the crew of the craft and had remembered something he had to do. The only person likely to question him would be Goldie, and he was safely installed at the helmsmen's briefing. There was no taking away and no putting back; simply the loosening and lifting of the cover at a point he would have earmarked as close to where the mainsheet was lying, and then the tying down again."

"Right," said Pedder. "I've got that. But I want to know why he put it on his own rope in his own boat?"

Masters drew out his pipe and started to pack it. "May I come to that later, sir?"

"All right. But you said he was expecting to kill off Maurice Hunt. He must have known by that time that Hunt wasn't crewing for Martin."

Masters sucked on the stem of his pipe to make sure it would draw. "That had me puzzled, too, sir. So I looked into it pretty carefully. Goldie came up on Saturday, arriving about midday. And that was after Martin and Cleveland had gone on the water. Goldie and Goatcher went out in the afternoon before *Spearhead* returned. Martin and Cleveland were away before *Slowcoach* returned to berth. So the crews did not meet on Saturday. That was easy enough to understand, but I was faced with accounting for the fact that,

191

on Sunday, Goatcher would see that it was Cleveland and not Hunt who was crewing for Martin. I thought I had fallen down over that one until I learned one very important fact."

"And what was that?"

"Hunt came down before the race on Sunday morning to see Harry Martin. They were quite friendly, and don't forget Hunt had agreed to crew for Martin until so-called business caused him to cry off. But more of that later. When Goatcher arrived to help Goldie get *Slowcoach* ready on Sunday morning, there was Hunt, doing various chores around *Spearhead*. True, there were three of them about the boat, but it seems obvious to me that Goatcher thought Jimmy was the third man. After all, the lists said Hunt was crewing for Martin. Goldie got away first, so Goatcher didn't see who was on the water with Martin."

"That disposed of the morning. What about when they returned in the afternoon?"

"The same thing. Harry Martin and Jimmy came in well up the fleet. Seventh or ninth, I believe. Goldie was a long way back. So *Spearhead* was virtually snugged down by the time *Slowcoach* got to its berth, and standing around with large cool drinks in their hands were Martin, Mandy Martin, the two Martin children, Jimmy and Maurice Hunt. Six of them. There was nothing there to suggest to Goatcher that Hunt was not crewing for Martin."

"So, believing Hunt was crewing for Martin, Goatcher went ahead with his plan of putting cyanide on his own rope in his own boat. I still don't get it."

Masters struck a match for his pipe.

"We've heard lots of bits of gossip over the past two days, sir. Some we have obviously to ignore. Ashley upset Mrs Clare Bascombe by becoming a bit too nosey about her affair with a man called Dicky Seabright. We interviewed early on a rather straight-laced woman called Vera Bartram who is hot on warning people about their moral misdemeanours but who, to do her justice, would not pass on to us anything she knew along those lines. And then Tip found something about another pair who were both married to other people but who ate their barbecue suppers in each other's arms behind the Sea Scout hut. And so on, sir. Even Sandy, who stuck pretty closely to the bars last night, thought he'd been transported to Peyton Place. He reckoned that every local person present was with somebody else's husband or wife. Right, Sandy?"

"When you say 'with', Chief, you must appreciate you're using a very general term."

Masters grinned. "It's not our business to be censorious unless it spills over into criminal activity, but it does do to show us all that under a seemingly calm surface here there is the devil to pay, at least in some quarters. I am pleased to say that all your reports from last night stress that for the most part it was a well-behaved gathering. But to get back to the mainsheet, sir. Not all the gossip we've heard has been about illicit relationships."

"No?"

"There has been mention of several small happenings. Two gentlemen named Alan and Tim, who sail together, were overheard in the showers complaining that somebody had deliberately damaged their trapeze wire, cutting it more than half way through so that it would deposit one or both in the water at the wrong time. A more elderly man called Barnaby discovered a two foot rent in a brand-new spinnaker. I have inspected both of these. There is no doubt in my mind that somebody had used hand pliers on the wire. It is very hard, plaited and strong, so ordinary pliers would not easily go through it, but they had gone half way through it. And the spinnaker. I found a single-edged razor blade lodged in the chute. It could have ripped the material to pieces. And, finally, Martin's mainsheet. When I first spoke to him about it, he told me that when he set out from London the rope was in perfect condition. He had used it as a boom lashing, so he supposed it must have rubbed on the journey up here. That may have been so, but these plaited terylene ropes don't chafe easily, and in any case it was still in good enough order to help *Spearhead* to a very good finishing position on Sunday. But, on Monday morning, it was in a bad

193

enough way for Jimmy Cleveland to borrow Goldie's mainsheet rather than trust his own. We've got the mainsheet in our possession, sir. As you will recall, Jimmy changed it while Martin returned to the hotel for his tools. Though the tools were removed at night, Martin, like most of the owners there, keeps a kit-bag holdall full of bits and pieces, and that stays in the boat overnight."

"What sort of bits and pieces?"

"Hanks of lashing rope, cleaning rags, grease for the hull and any old thing they have had to renew from time to time. Jimmy put the old rope in there. We have examined it closely. It is our opinion that the rope was almost cut through in two places, not by chafing, but by a sharp cutting tool . . ."

"Like a single-edged razor blade," interposed Green.

"You are saying somebody made sure that Martin and Jimmy could not use that rope on Monday, and to disguise the cutting of it, the perpetrator slightly damaged the equipment of several other craft. Sort of camouflage to suggest some sort of campaign against the fleet as a whole?"

"Precisely, sir. There were other incidents like those I've told you of. But we are satisfied that none is the act of the usual vandal. No covers were ripped or boats sprayed with slogans."

"Not a very clear attempt then?"

"I think it was clever, sir. He wanted to keep it low key, to give the impression that there was a spoiler about perhaps trying to pull off silly practical jokes, or to nobble the boats in the races, but not serious enough to arouse so much interest and annoyance that the Race Committee would have to take action. In other words, he didn't want it to become a talking point, though he reckoned he couldn't afford just one incident to make it appear that *Spearhead* was the sole object of his attention."

"I get it," said Pedder.

"So Goatcher knew that after discovering that their mainsheet was totally useless for Monday's race, Martin and Hunt would either have to borrow another one or scratch. Scratching was unlikely, he knew, because the boats are here

194

to race. The obvious source from which to borrow the rope in the short time they would have between discovering the damage and having to get on the water was from the boat next in line to theirs. They knew *Slowcoach* was not racing. Goldie, who is a fairly senior executive in a packaging firm, on the design side, had to make a call on a biggish customer in Newcastle who was demanding a new pack for some product or another. It was a question of business before pleasure. It was his absence, announced on Saturday, I believe, that helped Goatcher to formulate his final plan."

"How, Chief?" asked Tip. "I mean he came up here intending to kill Hunt. He brought the cyanide with him. He must have known what he was going to do and had made preparations."

"Difference between strategy and tactics, love," grunted Green. "He knew his objective all right, but the way of going about achieving his ends was a matter of opportunity."

"I agree with that," acknowledged Masters. "I suspect the original plan was to impregnate the genuine *Spearhead* mainsheet with the cyanide. However, I suspect that on Sunday, when there were five or six people clustered round *Spearhead* as it was being snugged down, Goatcher overheard some comment about the mainsheet being damaged and Martin's agreement to go to the chandler's van—which had attended on Sunday afternoon, remember—and buy a new one.

"My guess is that Goatcher thought a new rope would be ideal for his purpose. Hunt would be killed by a new rope, and if it was ever discovered how he was killed, all suspicion would be centred on the chandler who had supplied it, or on the manufacturer who had supplied him."

"Clever thinking, Judder."

"But Martin came back and announced that the chandler hadn't got the suitable rope on his van and would bring it on Monday afternoon. If Goatcher overheard that . . ."

"Which he would make bloody certain he did," interjected Pedder.

"Quite. With that knowledge, he had to alter his plans

somewhat. Quite simply, it would be easy to damage *Spearhead*'s mainsheet beyond usefulness for Monday's race, and to impregnate that belonging to *Slowcoach* in the almost certain knowledge that it would be borrowed for the race. This had other merits in Goatcher's eyes. Namely, that he would be absent from Abbot's Haven all day and thus, in his opinion, removed from all involvement in the death. He made sure he wouldn't be here to offer the rope to Hunt and Martin, or to give them permission to use it should they ask. He would, in fact, be far away and totally uninvolved with somebody borrowing, without permission, a piece of equipment which killed them when used. So no suspicion could fall on him."

"Until George Masters happened along," said Pedder. "Tell us how you got on to him, Judder."

"Framework," answered Masters. "I suspect Sandy and Ashley were a bit bemused at some of the things I asked them to do, but nobody can make bricks without straw, so I had to have a dump of raw material at my disposal." He turned to the chart. "You've already glanced at this, sir, and the others know what it is about. For instance, the yellow markings indicate those who mouth their mainsheets. We initially identified eleven, thinking our intended victim would be among them. When we learned that Hunt was to have crewed in *Spearhead* and that he is a mouther, too, we could add him below Jimmy's name and paint him yellow."

"So he entered the frame?"

"Yes. Similarly, the red markings show those who have been abroad in the fairly recent past. There are quite a few of them, as you see. I originally asked Sandy to provide information about holidays, then, just as we added Hunt to the mouthers, we added business trips to the list. And this netted Goatcher. We knew he had been away from the club, of course, because he did not know Jimmy had taken over from Hunt. Sandy learned Goatcher had been to Africa—to Zambia, to be precise.

"Then the blues indicate occupations that might conceivably bring people into contact with cyanide. There are not many of them, as you can see. Four was the initial count. This information was apparently useless until we started matching occupations to trips abroad."

Sandy Finch interrupted. "It wasn't 'we', Chief Constable. It was DCS Masters alone who sussed this one. I had Goatcher down as a civil servant. Which he is. But the Chief said ordinary civil servants don't normally go on business trips abroad. So he asked me to find out what sort of a civil servant Goatcher was."

"And?"

"He is in the Department of Trade and Industry, sir. Nothing startling in that. But he's in the Minerals and Metals Division, Copper Branch."

"Go on, Sandy."

"The Chief had wanted to know who had to deal with metal extractions and that sort of thing, and who had been abroad and so on. My enquiries gave us the information that Goatcher's trip to Zambia had been to Ndola and Chingola in the copper belt. On government business, of course."

"Of course. And in the big copper belt of Zambia they presumably use scads of cyanide for metal refining, extracting and so forth."

"That's it, sir. Quite what the processes are, I haven't yet been able to find out, but the prosecution will be able to work up quite a bit on the availability of cyanide in the fields Goatcher visited."

"No doubt. He just smuggled it in, did he?"

"Easy enough for a ranking civil servant with a locked government briefcase with the monarch's monogram stamped on it in gold," said Sandy. "Customs men recognize their own kind."

"As you say, easy enough. Thanks, Sandy." Pedder turned to Masters. "Right, Judder, you've given us means, method, opportunity, mechanics and all the rest of it. What about motive?"

"As you can see, sir, Goatcher was getting quite a lot of coloured marking. And there's yet one more to come. Pale green."

197

"Symbolizing what?"

"Actually, sir, we had again to make inclusions in our markings. Green was to indicate those indulging in what Bill calls side-swiping. Later on, we had to include in this category those who were the victims of side-swiping. The aggrieved parties, if you like. For instance, Mrs Goatcher and Hunt were green because of their affair. But Goatcher himself didn't figure, until we altered the qualifications, as it were. Then Goatcher won himself yet another stripe.

"We knew Hunt was a womanizer, and our first information about him, winkled out by Bill and later confirmed by Ashley, was that he had taken on Nancy Claybourn, the pretty little wife of a business competitor up here in Wearbay. We heard nothing about Mrs Goatcher having an affair with Hunt. I, personally, was lucky enough to get the first hint of it. I had been given a verbal description of Hunt, and then on Tuesday afternoon, whilst I was waiting for Berger to bring the car back from Wearbay, I went under a tree at the end of the camp site to get out of the sun. I suppose I was virtually hidden from sight in the shade, and as far as I could see the site was deserted. But after a few minutes I saw a man, who I thought must resemble Hunt, come out of a caravan. The woman kissed him on the step. She then glanced about her furtively as if to make sure they had not been seen while the man made an equally furtive get-away up the bank and through the bushes at the back of the van. It had all the hallmarks of an assignation; I believed the man to be Hunt; I was almost certain the woman could not have been Nancy Claybourn—she would not have had a van on the site; and it was at that time in the afternoon when the first of the fleet could be expected to start returning. So I guessed that the husband was on the water, and during his absence the wife and Hunt had been side-swiping.

"It was easy enough to identify the woman from the van. It belonged to Mr and Mrs Goatcher."

"So Goatcher and his missus got a green stripe apiece and Hunt got a second one?"

"That's it, sir. Now we have to come back to the very moral

198

Vera Bartram. I tackled her this afternoon on my own. I explained, as far as I felt wise, the very serious stage our investigation had reached and appealed to her, despite her reservations, to help us find Jimmy's murderer. I said I particularly wished to know about the liaison between Hunt and Mrs Goatcher. I was very careful not to mention Goatcher himself, because until she should know I regarded him as a murderer, she regarded him as an innocent and injured party. So I stressed that it was Hunt's part in the drama I was keen to hear about. She co-operated very well. She had to compare murder with moral laxity. Murder is the greater sin, therefore she forgot her principles and talked about the lesser sin in order to confound the greater.

"I will not bother with all we got from her except one point, and that is she was able to prove Goatcher knew of the liaison between his wife and Hunt. The affair has been going on for some time, apparently. As Hunt does not sail the same class of boat as Goatcher, he can often be ashore in Mrs Goatcher's company when her husband is afloat. The van is actually hers. She bought it and insists on towing it wherever it is they are sailing. Goatcher, as a crew, does not have a boat to tow, so he can have no objections on those grounds, although events have proved that he might have objected for other reasons.

"Vera Bartram suggested Hunt had cried off the racing as Martin's crew as soon as he heard that the Goatchers were definitely attending the meeting. Earlier on, the business trip to Zambia had not been finally fixed, but once it became obvious that Goatcher would be back in time to crew for Goldie, Hunt withdrew from crewing for Martin so that he and Mrs Goatcher would have chance to be together each race day. And that provides the motive, sir. Jealousy over infidelity I suppose you would call it.

"Sandy and Ashley will have one or two things to finalize, but other than that, I think the case is complete, sir. You will notice on the chart that Goatcher has, in fact, won most of the coloured Brownie-points and there's one big gold star still waiting to go alongside his name."

"What's that?" asked Pedder.

"I know," said Berger excitedly.

"What, son?"

"Propinquity, sir."

"What the hell does that mean?"

"All yesterday and today," said Berger, "the Chief has been mentioning propinquity. He's been saying that closeness on the dinghy park was going to be important."

"Meaning what exactly?"

"I think it was a feeling the Chief had, sir. He gets them sometimes."

"So I've noticed."

Masters grinned. "All I felt was that this operation would have been extremely difficult if *Spearhead* and *Slowcoach* had been at opposite ends of the dinghy park. For instance, Jimmy Cleveland wouldn't have borrowed a mainsheet from a dinghy two hundred yards away. Goatcher would have found it more difficult to cut a rope in a boat a long way away from the spot where he could legitimately operate. And so on."

"What if they had been far apart?" asked Pedder.

"They couldn't have been, sir," interposed Tip. "They allocated block-bookings to each club. Goatcher knew that he could never have been more than five places from *Spearhead*. And even if he hadn't been, the Chief would have altered the gold Brownie-star, just as he did the other colour qualifications, so that propinquity would include whatever distance the two were apart."

Everybody laughed, including Masters.

"Well said, lass," chuckled Green. "I shall call you Mrs Thornburgh from now on."

"Mrs Who?"

"No, petal, not Mrs Who. Surely you know what Mrs Humphry Ward said in *Robert Elsmere*?"

"I'm afraid I don't. Should I?"

"The quote goes: 'Propinquity does it—as Mrs Thornburgh is always reminding us'."

"I see."

"I do, too, Bill," said Pedder getting to his feet. "Well,

Judder, you've pulled it off again with your airy-fairy nonsense methods. So what, now? Can I buy you all a drink?"

"That would be most acceptable, sir, but if you would excuse us, Bill and I are still on holiday and our wives will be wanting us to get back as soon as possible. And Sergeants Tippen and Berger are joining us for supper, although this is the first they've heard of it."

"I thought that's what you'd say, so we won't hold you up. But thanks for everything."

The two cars returned to Stanhope in convoy, Masters leading with Green in the Jaguar, Berger and Tip in the official Yard Rover. As the Jaguar nosed gently down the hill towards the cottage a minute or two before eight, Green suddenly sat up straight. "She's there," he breathed. "Look, George, Nel's there."

"I see her, Bill."

"The little beauty!"

As they left the car, the cottage door opened. Wanda and Doris came out. Wanda was carrying the packet of ovals.

"I thought you'd need these, William."

"Ta, love." He kissed Doris and then turned to Nel who had slowly wagged her way across the road towards him.

"I knew exactly when you'd finished the case, darling," said Wanda as she kissed her husband.

"Oh, how?"

"I was at the window when Nel came down the hill. She seemed to know William had finished whatever business was keeping him away."

"You mean Nel thinks he deserted her and not vice versa?"

"Yes. Just look at them."

There was no doubt about it. Though he was making much of her, it was Nel that was welcoming Green home.